The Empire of Arkania

The Avat Prince

VOLUME EIGHT

Copyright © 2024 Myranda V. Peterson

Cover art and interior illustrations © Myranda V. Peterson
House MVP Logo © House MVP
The Avat Prince: Tales of Arkania Skits © House MVP

Cartography brushes used in map artwork designed by Joel Pigou
https://www.gumroad.com/joelpigou

ISBN 9781957330129

First Edition Printed October 2021
MVP TV Edition Printed November 2024

Printed by IngramSpark in the USA.

House MVP
16 Thomas Patten Dr., P.O. Box 21
Randolph, MA, 02368

https://www.housemvpmedia.com

The text of this book is set in 12-point Adobe Garamond Pro.

For those who believe in the impossible.

The Avat Prince

Volume Eight

WRITTEN AND ILLUSTRATED BY

MYRANDA V. PETERSON

TALES OF ARKANIA

To access locked skits for
THE AVAT PRINCE:

First, get reading!

When you see the word 'TV' at the end of a
sentence, it's time for a skit!

Illustrations are paired off with these pages.
Scan an illustration's QR code to access its skit.

Enter the password.

Enjoy the show!

(Don't forget to come back to keep reading the story!)

MVP

BOSTON
MVP
est. 1994
HOUSE MVP

PREVIOUSLY IN
THE AVAT PRINCE...

Brent's talk with Councilman Qëmzhi connects his visions with stories of Zion the Hero, and reveals that the head council made a deal with the 'Elder' that would protect them from "dragons and serpents". But how much of this is true — and how much is a result of Qëmzhi's aging mind?

Time goes on and, with the intelligence scouts going silent, Renée and her fellow graduates are left to take on odd jobs across the village. She soon joins Brent and Liam in escorting Harver to Heletia Cavern for engineering materials.

Meanwhile, Aaron chases leads on the missing scouts and discovers the ruins of a supporter's home. According to the imperial sign that's hammered into the yard, they were of the Lecil family and were caught hiding Avats.

In Heletia, Brent and the others have a close call with an entelodon and are saved by Mekial, who gets injured. Renée insists that he see the healer, Khirsta, but on visiting her it becomes clear that he's actually unharmed. Khirsta suggests that he see an aetherist to learn what could've happened.

Later, Aaron is debriefed by Ivan and shares that not even their supporters know what happened to the scouts. But, he did learn that an entire region has been locked down after an attack by "Saruke's Shade". The criminal intrigues Aaron, for on his wanted posters it's clear that his mask bears the Liberation Fronts' insignia. Ivan claims that the mask once belonged to a supporter, but he doesn't know who wears it now.

Aaron also adds that Empyrean's Guard suspects Odelwhite Forest is Taranis' hideout, and they may stage an attack.

Meanwhile, Mekial asks Kro to help him learn if he's an aetherist. Kro challenges him to meet outside of the valley — to their misfortune, Empyrean's Guard strikes their meetup spot.

Accompanied by the missing intelligence scouts, Saruke's Shade witnesses this. Donning his feral mask, he readies his sword.

60

MEKIAL SLIPPED INTO a hollow space beneath a hilled path and nestled close to the bushes that were there.

His friends followed him, crushing their bodies against his as they piled into the tiny area. They nearly stopped breathing when a storm of metal feet rushed along the hill above. A short moment later, they stopped.

"Did you see where they went?" they heard a man inquire after a tense lapse of silence.

Lacey let slip a pale whimper.

Klarys muffled it.

"We lost them through the trees," another guardsman replied bitterly.

"They looked small," one of them recounted. "Like children."

"They're probably stolen slaves," the first one concluded. "Stay on your toes. Those savages have slaughtered more men than I care to count in the last few weeks. If you don't keep your guard up, you might just lose your head in cold blood."

Mekial and all of his friends exchanged sharp, inquisitive looks. They refused to breathe.

"Check down that way," the group leader carried on. "Give a shout if you find something."

"Sir."

"You two, check there."

He must've pointed, for the rest of the guardsmen that had arrived scattered back into the woods without a word.

Fortunately, none of them came down to where the children were.

"Guess we really lost them now," Klarys breathed, sensing they were safe. She let go of Lacey, who sighed shakily.

"What savages' hideout?" Lilian asked, looking between her older friends anxiously. "Do savages hide in these woods?"

"No," Dillon answered, absently listening to the imperial officers as they got further away. "It sounds like they might be looking for Taranis. Mom says that's what they call us."

"But we're not savages!"

"We haven't sent out any raiders at all this past month," Mekial muttered, stuck on what the first guardsman had said. "But then… who killed the people they were talking about?"

None of his friends responded. The guardsman's story was a mystery to them all.

"I hope Kro's okay," Kurt said, breaking the silence.

"Me, too," Lilian added sadly.

"He helped us get away," Dillon recounted absently, "but, after that explosion…" He stopped, cutting himself off. It was a moment before he spoke again. "Yeah. I hope he's okay, too."

Mekial scowled at his hand and flexed his fingers before closing them into a tight fist.

Maybe if he'd learned how to control the aether, he could've helped Kro.

Kurt gulped and looked between his friends' morbid faces. "What now?"

"Lacey?" Klarys had rested a hand on the girl's shoulder when she noticed she was trembling all over.

Though she was staring at the undergrowth, Lacey's gaze was unfocused and her hands were glued to her head. "There's a lot of them…" she whispered tearfully. "There's so many soldiers…I can hear them…everywhere…!"

Klarys exchanged looks with everyone else, clearly nervous.

"There's too many…" Lacey's face contorted with fear. "We're not gonna make it…"

"Don't say that, Lace." Dillon reached around Kurt to touch her arm and though she looked up with a jolt, he kept a straight face. "We're gonna —"

The approaching roar of fire rang in his ears.

"Get down!" he yelled, throwing his arms around everyone near him, and they all curled against the hill just as a surge of fire devoured a crowd of trees opposite them.

Clambering away from the spreading heat, they scrambled back into the open.

"There's another one coming!" Lilian cried and upon spotting a glimmer of light tearing through the trees, she and all those with her dove to avoid another wave of flames.

Like the one before it, the storm of fire swallowed underbrush and low branches with a terrifying growl and raced to the treetops in search of more fuel. One of the trees cracked noisily, its bark splintering, and with an agonized moan it began to lean, all of its weight threatening to crush the children in one blow.

"Run!" Dillon shouted and he and the others scrambled out of the tree's path, leaving it to crash into a sea of bushes. Sparks erupted, blown out by the force of the collapse, and within seconds all of the shrubs were alight.

When Dillon and the others had gotten a fair distance away, they snatched a look back and learned that the currents of fire and the burning leafage had formed a great wall of crackling timber behind them. As if that weren't enough, smoke was beginning to curl off of the smoldering forestry, its vaporous form rising to drown the sky in a muddy haze.

The stench of blazing wood swelled around it, stinging the children's eyes and burning their nostrils, and although they knew they needed to find escape they could see no such salvation in any direction. Fire barred them on one side and a countless number of imperials blocked them on the other. They'd need a miracle to get out of the forest alive.

Only Kurt managed to clamber through that stiflingly sober truth and emerge on the other side with an idea.

"We should use your distress signal!" He grabbed Mekial by the arm and his attention with it. "We can use it to let everyone in

Taranis know we're in trouble! Maybe they'll send someone to save us!"

It seemed like a good plan, Mekial believed at first.

But in the next few seconds he had to think about it, it lost all sense of reliability. Even if someone saw the signal, it'd take them hours to cross the whole valley and make it this deep into the forest. A horse might cut that time in half and a saiga even more so, but...

"Just let me do it!" Kurt interrupted, seeing his reservation, and he lunged for Mekial's bag.

"Stop!" Mekial stepped out of his way.

Dillon snatched Kurt's arm.

"We can't!" Dillon told him. "If we shoot something into the sky, we could let the guardsmen know where we are!"

"But if we don't try to call for help we'll end up dead or caught by them anyway! There's nowhere for us to go!" Kurt yanked himself free and to everyone's surprise, he managed to tear the engineer's tool out of Mekial's bag.

Lacey stepped forward, looking like she wanted to stop him, but she clearly wasn't sure how.

"Wait!" Mekial tried to recover it. "Dillon's right, we can't —!"

"Give it back!" Dillon added at the same time, going for the tool.

"We can't just keep running —!" Kurt fought back.

They wrestled over it, each one trying to rip it from the others' grasp until one of their hands — they weren't sure whose — slid along its edge and smacked off its bottom piece.

Triggered by that single displacement the main shaft rattled, offset by the rising pressure of what it contained.

The boys' arms shook along with it, none of them able to keep a firm hold on it until, with a blast of light and a violent downward motion, a sizzling flare thundered out of its head and whizzed into the sky.

All of the children gaped at it, wide-eyed as the beacon took off in a blaze of green glory.

Finally, Dillon found his voice. "Uh-oh," he breathed.

"Over here!"

The children whirled; Lacey hid behind Klarys with a terrified yelp.

Guardsmen broke through the trees before them.

⟡

Breathing raggedly, Kro stared into the flaming roof of the forest. Battered and bruised and his clothes in tatters, he found that he barely had the strength to get off the ground. The stifling air made him even more uncomfortable, blasting him with unyielding heat as the surrounding flames inched ever closer to his location.

With hooded eyes, he strained to control his breathing.

In…

Out…

In…

He wondered if Mekial and the others had made it away safely. They should've — his shield, while not nearly as strong as one that Tyre could've made, had withstood the guardsman's second attack. The only thing was that on impact, the blast had severed Kro's link with the aether and left him all but unconscious.

As unfortunate as he knew it to be, he also knew that it made sense. The barrier's abrupt destruction had rippled back to him through the aether, affecting the very physical state of his being. It'd probably be a few hours, perhaps longer, before he could connect with it again.

Kro replayed it all in his head: the way the flames had encased the imperial's body, the force of the aether's touch when he'd first connected with it…

It was all so wrong. No one should be able to handle that sort of connection with the aether. A connection that was so powerful they could encase their body in an element as dangerous as fire. It was impossible. It only existed in stories. Legends.

Plays.

Nevertheless, that didn't change how gruesome it had felt to sense that guardsman's aetherial connection. In every way, his link had seemed unnatural.

Artificial.

Kro tried moving his hand.

His fingers twitched.

Good.

He didn't have time to brood. He didn't know where Mekial or any of the boy's friends were. He could only hope that they weren't in imperial hands.

For now, he couldn't think about it. As much as he didn't like to admit it, he couldn't do anything for them anymore.

But he could do one thing for the people of Taranis.

"C…come on…Kro…" Breathing shallowly, it took almost all of his strength to lift his right arm and point his finger into the sky. He grabbed his bicep to hold it steady. "C…come on…it's your time…to play the hero…!"

His eyes tightened.

He grabbed the aether — albeit loosely — and redirected it back at himself. A gentle wind expanded around him, brushing dry leaves and twigs away, and a soft light of pink and violet coursed around him.

He took another breath and held onto it for dear life.

A blast of dark light shot out of his fingertip and roared into the billowing sky.

He smiled weakly, proud of his accomplishment, and let his arms flop back to the ground. The aetherial light around him vanished.

His breathing was hoarser now. With his strength waning, he let his head roll to the side. His vision began to fur.

Before his mind slipped into nothingness, he saw a pair of black-clad feet step through the flames and approach him. Whether it was due to his own fading consciousness or not, he noticed that he could hardly hear the stranger's approach at all.

Maybe it was just a hallucination.

The man knelt before him, one gloved hand extended in an offer of help.

But Kro blacked out before he could take it.

Taranis was in all but an uproar when Brent, Aaron and Eklaire returned to it. Everywhere villagers were ushering their children to get inside, fearful of what the black smoke might mean, and the main road was crowded with people facing the valley. Many of them were gaping at the darkness or pointing it out to friends nearby as they murmured to one another, their terror clear.

"Is it the Empire?"

"What're we gonna do?"

"Did something happen to the scouts after all?"

"That's a lot of smoke…"

Brent slowed to a stop behind them, his golden eyes pinned to the smoke as it stretched to haze the skyline. His jaw tightened.

"The chief already dispatched the border scouts to put it out," he caught someone near the stream telling another villager. "They took the saigas and most of the horses."

"That's a relief," Aaron murmured, overhearing the man's words as well.

"Brent! Aaron!"

At the sound of their names, Brent and Aaron turned to face the upper half of the main road.

Harver was jogging towards them. Renée was with her, her sword belted to her side.

"Hey." Brent turned to face them as they closed in. "Anyone know what happened out there? Why're you armed?" He added, spotting Renée's weapon.

"The chief wanted all of the raiders and scouts to arm themselves as a precaution," Harver answered and she cast Renée a short, worried look. "We haven't gotten any other orders though, so I've been trying to help Renée find Mekial."

"Mekial?" Brent frowned and looked at Renée. "Why? Isn't he at the sparring hall?"

"I already checked there. And the schoolhouse," Renée said. She spoke fast — she was clearly nervous. "My parents and I haven't seen him since last night. When I woke up his bed was empty, so

I just thought he went to the sparring hall before his schoolhouse lessons like he always does. But, Jeffrey said he didn't go to training today, and Yulia didn't see him, either. Have you?"

"No." Brent looked at Aaron and Eklaire.

Aaron shook his head.

Eklaire, clutching her basket of Arkanian prunes, did the same.

Renée's brow creased further and her shoulders sank.

Brent searched the road for anyone else they could ask and soon spotted Liam making his way up the hill.

His silver eyes were narrowed to a squint as he scanned the path and he kept craning his neck and peering over shoulders as if he were on the hunt for something. Similar to Renée and a few other villagers along the road his weapons were equipped, consisting of his sword on his back and his knife against his left thigh.

Brent called out to him and Liam drifted towards their group, but it didn't seem like he'd actually heard his name. In fact, he was still preoccupied with his search.

"Lose something?" Brent frowned.

Liam finally noticed them. "Any of you seen Lilian?" he asked. "I've been looking for her since the smoke went up, but I can't find her."

Brent's skin prickled with unease. "She's gone, too?"

Liam frowned. "What do you mean, 'too'?"

"Dillon? Dillon!"

Brent and those with him faced the opposite side of the stream in time to catch Eve running out from between a pair of houses. Her fear was evident. "Has anyone seen Dillon?!"

"I can't find Klarys, either!" another woman told her, her tightly-coiled hair and dark skin resemblant of the child she was related to. "And I heard from Elma that Lacey is gone, too. So is Kurt!"

"All of them?" Eklaire whispered nervously.

Aaron's stark frown hardened and it barely broke when a flash of green light glinted in the distance. He looked up.

Another villager pointed it out from elsewhere. "What's that?"

With the break of quiet that had settled across the road after the mothers' display of despair, all ears heard the notification and all eyes searched until they spotted a glowing light tearing out of the woods.

It climbed still higher as the villagers watched it, its blaze leaving a trail of jade smoke through the shifting black. When it finally peaked, it erupted. Fire and cinders blew out of the explosion like Harver's fireworks, their light glancing off of the haze, and then they twinkled out of sight as they fell back to the forest.

Brent's eyes creased with confusion. "What was that?"

"That…was Isaac's prototype!" Harver pointed at the winking cinders, her mouth agape. An instant later, she looked horribly confused. "But how'd it even get out there…?"

"What kind of prototype?" Liam asked.

"We've been upgrading tools for raiders to use as distress signals," Harver replied. "We're still in the developing stages, and I think that one was Isaac's design. But…" She stared at the smoke again, where Isaac's light show had long-since vanished. "It was stored in the engineers' workshop…"

"Then someone must've snatched it," Brent deduced. "Was it the aetheriests with border patrol?"

"I don't think they would've had the time. They left too fast. They wouldn't have needed it anyway, since they're aetheriests."

Brent paused, frowning.

If it wasn't the aetheriests and the only other villagers who weren't around were Mekial and his friends, then…

His heart dropped.

Renée covered her mouth, her growing eyes fixed on the smoke as she came to the same realization. "Mekial…!"

Liam's normally narrow eyes widened as well.

"Then him and the other kids're out there?" Eklaire was panicked. "All of them?!"

She flinched when something else burst out of Odelwhite with a resounding pop.

She and everyone else on the main road looked again, and this time watched as a ball of dark light ascended into the dismal sky. It hung in the air upon the apex of its ascent, idle, and then it exploded, highlighting the billowing clouds with a temporary blast of white.

The quiet that settled over the road shook Harver to her core.

She looked around at everyone.

Brent stared, wishing it wasn't real.

But it was.

After all these years…

Having just vacated the conference room in the Main House, Ivan stared out of the dining hall's windows in just as much disbelief.

Xëri stepped forward to join him, and she placed a hand on his arm.

Her touch drew him out of his despair. Dogged determination took its place.

"Wh…what was that?" Harver took a step back, wary. She tried looking at her friends for an answer, but none of them would turn from where the dark light had been, as if they'd been frozen.

Around her, the other villagers were just as confused and just as afraid.

Brent shared a grave look with Aaron.

"Everyone!"

Heads turned to see Ivan and Xëri standing at the crest of the hill, pillars of hope and stability.

It was Xëri who'd spoken. "Get inside, and lock your doors!"

"Raiders!" Ivan bellowed. "Defensive positions!"

"Wh-what's going on?" Harver stammered, stepping out of peoples' way as they moved to fulfill the orders.

"It was a signal."

Harver looked at Liam, whose face was hard and bleak.

He glared at the distant firestorm. "Imperials are invading the valley."

Horror took Harver's face.

Renée set a steely gaze on the horizon.

Eklaire looked out anxiously.

"Then we'll fight 'em off." Brent set his golden eyes of resolve on the blazing skyline. "And we're gettin' Mekial and the others outta there."

61

LIAM NODDED IN agreement with Brent. He already looked like he was ready to sprint for the woods at that very moment.

Aaron wasn't as eager. "How?" he returned. While he was just as troubled by the children's plight, he seemed to be even more annoyed with Brent's evident lack of forethought. "The aetheriests took all the saigas we had to get out there, and if we tried to use horses it'd take us too long!"

Brent turned on him. "What are we s'posed to do, wait here?!"

"Hey, wait! *Wait!*" Harver broke in between them, keeping them apart. "I think…" She hesitated, but at their pressing looks she went on: "I think I've got something that can help you get out there."

They waited.

"I've only been able to run a few tests with it, and I'd rather make a few more adjustments," she confessed, "but at this point, it's all we've got." She looked between them. "Well? It's up to you."

Brent and Aaron looked at one another.

Liam came forward.

"Where is it?" he demanded.

Harver shot a bracing look from him to the others.

"This way," she said and she took all of them, including Eklaire, to her backyard.

Along the trees that lined it, a patterned blanket was spread out

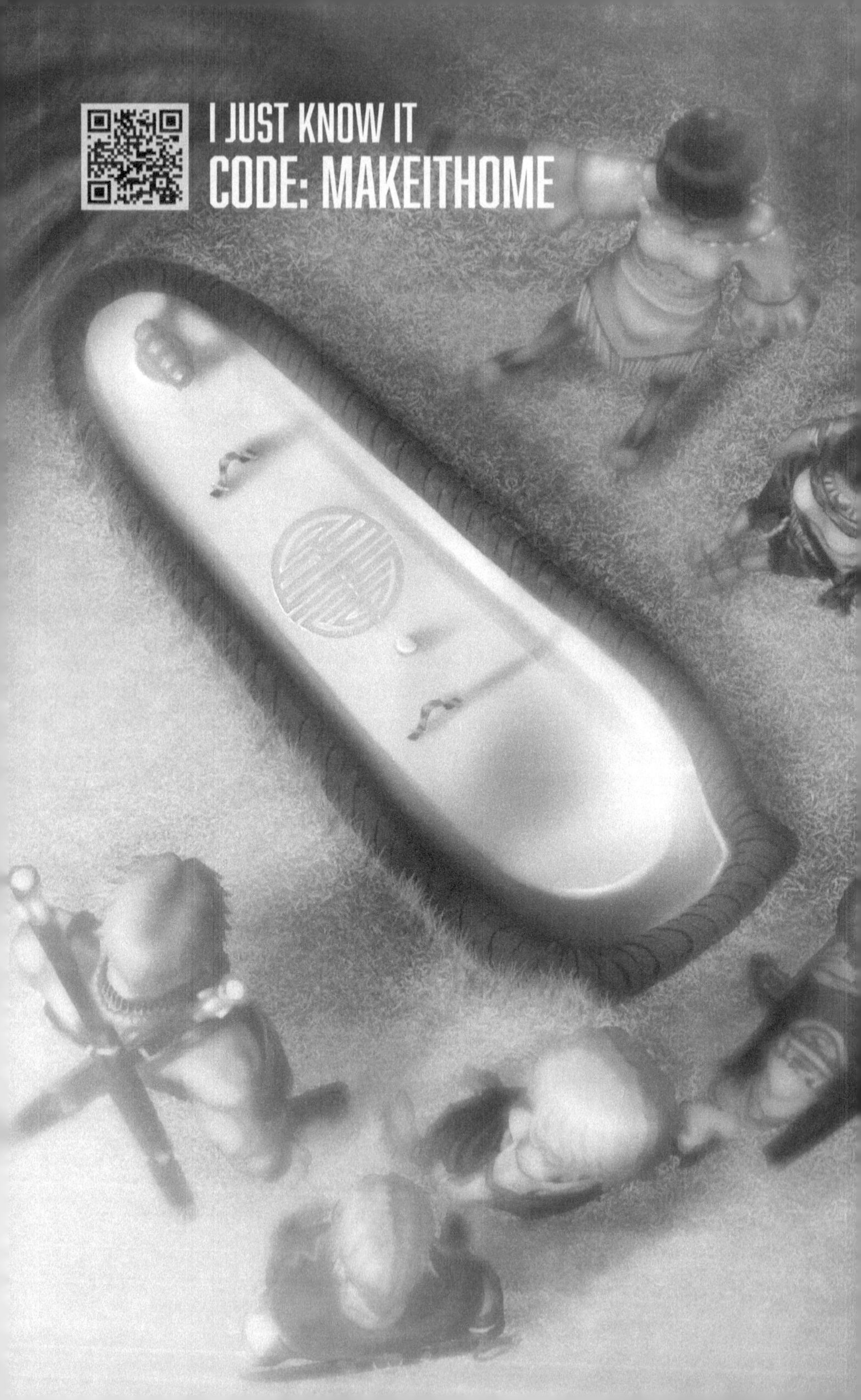

I JUST KNOW IT
CODE: MAKEITHOME

on top of something. Its immediate shape and purpose were impossible for her friends to determine, but they could at least tell that it stood about four or five inches off the ground.

Gathering near, they waited for Harver to uncover it and explain.[tv]

"I was gonna make a really big show of these since I've been working on them for so long," Harver said as she came nearer to them, "but, I guess now's as good a time to show them off as any."

Seizing one of the blankets, she ripped it back.

A long board that was crafted into a streamlined shape was revealed to the group, its gleaming face edged with a thick barrier that consisted of a rubbery, blue material. This same rubbershroom texture was grafted onto the handle at the front of the platform, offering it a spongey but firm grip.

Foot straps were welded onto the deck as well and upon closer examination, it could be seen that the Liberation Fronts' emblem of interlocking and disconnected rings was engraved between them.

"You guys remember how I needed to get qazhë seeds a while back, right?" Harver asked, looking between her friends, and when they nodded she continued: "The ones I grabbed were spares, but I already had some that I brought to the Luminoro Watch, for one of them to bless it.

"When a Luminoro touches certain objects, it's able to bless them with its own access to the aether." Harver tossed the patterned blanket aside and circled around the silver boards. "Qazhë seeds specifically link up with the quintessence in the air, and can absorb and expel large quantities of it at a steady rate."

She completely lost her train of thought. "I wasn't really sure how many seeds to use in the beginning, to be honest, and there was the issue of figuring out the mechanics of propulsion, so these things were pretty awkward to use at first. The handle was too, now that I think about it…the aerodynamics were pretty tricky. And —"

"Harver!" Brent interrupted and she jumped. "We need to get to Odelwhite *now*. How're these…*things*…s'posed help us?"

Harver's mouth hung open for a second, as if she didn't know how to respond.

Finally, she settled for something simple: "They fly."

Brent didn't look like he believed her.

Liam was just as skeptical.

Renée and Aaron's mouths fell open.

"They *what?*" Eklaire's whole head seemed to drop.

"Look." Kneeling, Harver seized the rearmost part of one of the boards and lifted it with both hands, revealing a small, box-like object that was attached underneath. A strange apparatus with rounded blades was fitted inside of it, pointing towards the back of the vehicle.

Her friends knelt for a better look.

"These propellers can push the board to speeds that even a saiga can't reach," Harver explained, pointing at the blades. "There's another set that's built directly into the platform" — she pointed at a closed vent on the board's underside — "and when it opens up, it allows air to enter the board and activate the qazhë seed, which absorbs the air and expels it, giving the board the push it needs to fly. As long as the underside propellers keep spinning to even out the airflow, these things can produce enough energy to suspend two people in midair for prolonged periods of time. Three if someone's small enough. The propellers in the back push the whole thing forward."

"Oh…my…" Eklaire covered her mouth.

"You mean these things can actually fly?!" Brent still couldn't believe it.

Harver stood with a nod, but it was stiff. "At least, they passed all of the flight tests. Their durability and endurance are still a bit shaky. But," she added, noticing their doubtful stares, "you can trust me when I tell you that these things can definitely get you to the forest before that fire gets any bigger. And hopefully, before anything bad happens to Mekial and the others."

The villagers exchanged looks.

"…If it's all we've got, then let's do it." Brent braved to stand atop the board Harver had lifted and hooked one of his feet into the front strap. It was well-balanced. "How does it work?"

"There're only a couple of buttons that operate it: the accelerator" — Harver indicated a button behind his rear foot — "and that's to turn it on and to make it ascend." She pointed at the button in the handle. "You have to roll the button in the handle *before* you press it every time you wanna turn the Skycraft on."

Brent's eyebrows twitched confusedly. "Skycraft?"

"That's what I call them." She waved a shooing hand. "Anyway, rolling it gets the underside propellers going. If you just push the button the vent leading to the qazhë seeds'll open, but without the fans to regulate it you'll just blast into the sky."

"I — blast into the —?" Brent didn't like the sound of that.

"Pressing the button in the handle and stomping on the accelerator at the same time will give you a good speed boost when you take off," Harver went on, missing his reaction completely. "The amount of pressure you apply to the accelerator controls your speed so the harder you press it, the faster you'll go. Naturally, doing the opposite will make you slow down. Once you're stationary, tap the handle's button twice to descend.

"Oh, and you don't have to keep your thumb on the button when you're flying," she added. "But tap it again when you're close to the ground and you'll land. After that, it'll turn off on its own."

Brent looked the vehicle over. It seemed like a lot to take in at once, but if he paraphrased all of Harver's instructions to himself, he understood.

Which only left one question: "How do I steer it?"

Harver pointed at the low-fitted handle. "Twist that ninety-degrees clockwise to unlock it and pull it up to a comfortable height, then ninety-degrees counter to lock it in place. Turning it left or right will tilt the Skycraft in that direction, but if you wanna go up you have to pull it back. I'd think it obvious but, if you wanna go down then you have to push it forward. The farther forward or backward you move it, the steeper your climb or descent."

Reaching down, Brent started to raise the handle. "You guys got all that?"

"Yeah." Aaron approached the second vehicle and stood atop it.

"All right…" Brent rubbed the button in his handle. "Then let's see what this thing can do."

He rolled the button first. Then, he pushed it.

Immediately gusts of wind erupted from his board's underside, blasting out with enough force to make it bounce.

Then, it started to rise.

It was a steady motion and as its self-made winds increased, the grass in Harver's yard began to bow. The humming of the underside fans became more apparent as it levitated and soon, it was expelling a breeze that was strong enough to make it look like he and the others were standing in a windy field. Even the trees along the edge of the yard waved, gearing up to wish him farewell.

It wasn't long before he was floating a good several feet off the ground.

Eklaire's mouth fell open all over again. "Well, slap me with bread and call me a sandwich…"

Even Liam looked astonished, as did Renée.

Brent grinned and with a confident nod to Aaron, the redhead turned on his own vehicle.

"This is gonna take some getting used to," he noted when the security of land left him.

"Don't think you guys are going alone." Having overcome his surprise, Liam marched forward. "I'm getting Lilian."

"And I'm gonna find Mekial," Renée added, joining him.

"'Course." Brent held his hand out to her and helped her aboard.

Liam joined Aaron.

"Remember, they're still in development," Harver added, her eyes shriveling in the winds that blew about them. "So don't be too reckless with them! Good luck!"

Eklaire shielded herself as well, one arm wrapped around her basket of fruit while the other acted as a barrier for her eyes. "Ya'll come back now, y'hear?! With all of 'em!"

"We plan to," Aaron said, fitting his front foot into the front-most strap.

Liam slid his own foot into the strap nearest to him and gripped Aaron's shoulders for balance.

Brent tossed his eyes to the smoky horizon.

The sky was still far from being torched by the glaring hues of sunset, but an early darkness was shrouding the space above the forest. The sun burned red behind it, hovering as a bloody circle, and with the base of the smog deepening to dirty black, it was easy to tell that the wildfire had risen in height and strength. It wouldn't be long before the entire valley was consumed by an unbreathable darkness next.

"We'll be back," he said and sliding his rear foot back, he slammed his heel on the accelerator. At the same time, he pushed the handle's button.

Instantly the Skycraft responded: the wind that had been breezing out of its underside increased, causing the entire aircraft to jump, and the underside fans spun faster, steadying the surge of wind that was by now tearing out of the vehicle with full force. Dirt, grass and loose soil shot into the air, buffeted by a growing whirlwind, and with their hair and clothes billowing Harver and Eklaire blocked their faces.

Then with another powerful eruption of air, Brent tore into the sky.

Aaron blasted off a split second after him.

When the wind finally settled, Harver and Eklaire swung around to see where they'd gone.

By the time they'd found them, the four were already shrinking to the size of tiny dots in the distance.

62

"COME ON, THIS way!" Mekial shouted, all the while dodging through brambles as he led his friends away from the guardsmen that hounded them.

Not one of his friends broke stride, though their breath was ragged, and when she slowed down for fatigue Klarys snatched Lacey's hand and forced her to keep up. All the while Dillon, Kurt and Lilian ran alongside them.

None of them dared to shoot even the smallest of glances over their shoulders, for fear that one misstep could render them prey to their pursuers. Still, it was getting hard for them to breathe and that made their sprint that much harder: the air had thickened, choked by a terrible smog that sought to fill their lungs, and the sun had been blotted out to the point where the only light available was that of the fires that raged further away.

More flames had swooped through the trees as they'd evaded the imperials, rushing in from nowhere to collide everywhere, and their lashing bodies promised a world of ash in replace of the smoky, hellish landscape.

Even for that reason alone the children desperately sought refuge, daring to believe that they could make it out and avoid the fiery fate that threatened them on all sides.

Their hopes were dashed when arrows started whizzing past them, launched from the crossbows of the guardsmen that were swiftly closing in.

"Go, go!" Mekial yelled, waving for his friends to follow him through the barrage, and in the span of an instant they had so many close calls that their survival could only be counted a miracle: Kurt tripped once and was nearly struck in the arm; Lilian fell flat on her face and Mekial was nearly killed going to get her; Dillon barely escaped capture when he skidded beneath a low branch, leaving an arrow-net to catch it instead of him.

Mekial looked back, hearing the hollow *smack* of the net's collision, and he caught sight of the guardsmen as Dillon scrambled back to his feet. His heart jolted with panic.

It wouldn't be long before they caught up.

No sooner had he thought that did one of the imperials give a shout and drop into a sinkhole that swallowed him up to his waist.

His comrades didn't stop for him. But when the depression cracked and expanded to swallow them, too, they had to.

Mekial gaped, surprised.

"Mekial!"

Spinning at Klarys' cry, Mekial saw that she and the others had gotten even further away.

After shooting the imperials one last, cautious look, he hurried to join them.

"Are they still behind us?" Klarys asked when he got close.

"No," he panted and when he tried looking back for them, swirls of cinder-filled smoke curtained his view. "They…they got stuck."

"In what?" Klarys was perplexed.

"Does it matter?" Dillon interjected and he continued running, encouraging the others to go after him.

Though they were no longer being pursued, they weren't relieved. It was no wonder, for now that they had a chance to examine where they were they realized that they were hopelessly lost: every tree looked as dark and threatening as the last and if fire didn't block their path in one place, a wall of coiling smoke did. The trails were gone, hidden beneath soot and dried grass, and the faded shadows of imperials flickered in the dark along with their resonating voices.

"What now…?" Dillon wondered when they managed to enter

what he guessed had once been a lush clearing. Haze was drifting through it, dotted with embers, and far beyond the black trees enclosing it there stood a great wall of fire. "Everything looks the same! Which way's that stupid barrier?!"

"Kurt?" Towards the back of the group Lilian took hold of Kurt's arm, troubled by his pale face and heavy breathing.

He didn't notice her touch, far too concerned with the growing strain of taking a simple breath. Shakily he raised one hand, meaning to clutch his chest, but before he could his eyes rolled and he collapsed.

"Kurt!" Lilian exclaimed and the panic in her cry alerted the others.

"What's wrong with him?!" Lacey asked, whirling.

"I don't know! He just fainted!" Lilian tried shaking him awake. "Kurt! *Kurt!*"

"It's his lungs!" Dillon dropped beside her and tilted his head so he could hear Kurt's panting. It was raspy and labored. "Khirsta said it before: sometimes it's really hard for him to breathe if he over-works himself."

"It must be the smoke!" Mekial figured out. "We've been running for a while…all the smoke probably made it worse for him!"

"So what do we do?!" Lilian cried, her eyes watering, and she and the others watched as Dillon lifted Kurt up and rolled him onto his back.

"I've got him," he said, Kurt's head and arms dangling over his shoulders, and he stood. "But we really need to get out of here. He won't last like this —"

He broke off with a shout that his friends shared when a wave of fire whipped across the clearing and walled them off on one side.

Hardly a second later, another blast of flames rushed in on the other.

"Get back!" Dillon roared and at the same time, the second wave tore across the clearing to collide with the first, sealing them inside a baking circle.

Screaming they huddled together, sweat sailing down their backs to cling to their dirtied clothes. Hot wind seared them on every side, forcing them to clench their eyes, and the bellowing flames dared to shatter their eardrums.

Mekial crouched over part of the group as if to shield them with his own body. His arms were spread, his fingers extended, and as his cloak flapped against his back he thought for sure that every square inch of his skin would be scorched in seconds.

He gritted his teeth and dug his heels into the ground, straining to bear it. But a grunt soon pushed through his teeth and bloomed into a loud cry.

All at once a cold snap tumbled around them, bursting from nowhere to whirl around he and his friends like a self-contained cyclone. It expanded quickly, blowing against the fires with an icy chill that forced them back.

Immediately the smoke cleared and the temperature dropped. Given respite, Mekial and his friends slowly looked up to find that although the fires still trapped them, they were now lashing far away enough for them to be able to breathe. The lingering chill of the sudden frost only helped.

"Wh-wh-what was that?" Lilian stammered, her breath escaping her as a thin mist that vanished as soon as it left her.

"I…" Mekial swallowed. "I don't know…"

His eyes flinched when a shadow danced on the other side of the flames directly opposite them.

He blinked, thinking it was his imagination, only to watch as the shadow solidified into the outline of a human being. The next thing he knew it reached forward and breached the fires with one arm.

Mekial's jaw dropped and he and his friends watched, wide-eyed, as the person's shoulder broke through the fires next, followed by his torso, then his leg, until finally an entire person had stepped through the fiery ring to join them inside of it.

It was a guardsman — and not a hair on him was burned.

Malice glowed in his dull gray eyes and his face was scarred and weathered. Saying nothing, he marched ever closer to the frightened children, sparks of fire shooting out of his heels with every step.

Without warning Lacey screamed, her sights elsewhere, and her friends turned in time to watch as another guardsman stepped through the flames, his crossbow already raised.

The first imperial finally stopped walking. Unlike his partner he carried no bow, but his large hand was planted atop his sword.

"Don't know which one of you decided to pull that trick," he said flatly, "but don't think you can get away with it again."

The children said nothing, their breath short.

"We'll take the devils," the man continued in that same, empty tone. "Savages can die here."

Wordlessly, his comrade aimed his crossbow at Klarys. His finger moved for the trigger.

Mekial leaped in front of her, knife in hand. Winding his arm back, he threw it so that it spiraled end over end and struck the man in the face.

The guardsman's head snapped back, and he accidentally pulled his crossbow's trigger. But instead of hitting his target, his arrow flew out of the fiery ring and into the blackness beyond.

Unsheathing his second knife Mekial swung to face the other imperial, who was already running at him with his sword drawn. As soon as he was close, the man pulled his sword back and drove it forward, meaning to impale the trainee.

But Mekial sidestepped the blow and, pulled by a strange, invisible force, the guardsman wound up thrusting his blade into the ground.

With the imperial's face now closer to him, Mekial stabbed his knife into the man's eye.

The imperial screamed and before he could back away, Mekial seized his sword by the hilt and slammed his feet into the man's chest, shoving him.

Mekial himself dropped as soon as they were apart, imperial sword in hand, and he twisted to find where the guardsman had gone.

As soon as he looked, the imperial stumbled and tripped in his direction, screaming over his wounded eye.

Yelling, Mekial unearthed the imperial's sword and braced its hilt against the ground. Its sharp blade went up as soon as the guardsman dropped towards him.

With the nauseating sound of pierced flesh, it impaled him.

When Mekial dared to open his scrunched eyes, he found himself panting before the bloody, one-eyed scowl of a dead guardsman.

Half of the fiery circle went out.

"Mekial!" Lilian shrieked and he swung to see that the other guardsman was already pointing his crossbow at him. He was also wounded, though not as terribly as his partner: Mekial's knife had only cut open his cheek.

As soon as he made eye contact with his would-be killer, the guardsman pulled the crossbow's trigger.

Mekial's eyes grew, his vision swallowed by the incoming arrow that made to shatter his skull. Petrified with the fear of a death he hadn't seen coming, he sat there in shock —

So it was that he watched in admirable stillness as the arrow veered off course by a fraction and whizzed past his cheek.

It didn't even scratch him.

The guardsman hastily made to load a new arrow but with his body coming back to life, Mekial moved faster: snatching a dagger out of the dead imperial's belt, he held it by its point and threw it.

It somersaulted the distance and crashed into the guardsman's brow. He crumpled instantly.

In the same instant, the other half of the fiery enclosure blew out.

Mekial sagged to his knees, gasping. His stomach did backflips.

Doubling over, he threw up.

"Mekial!" Lilian ran to him.

Panting, Dillon looked from one dead guardsman to the other. He didn't know whether to be relieved or sick.

Lacey clung to his sleeve, terrified.

Once sure that he'd upended everything that he'd ever eaten, Mekial sat up breathlessly. Wiping his mouth, he withstood the urge to dry-heave next.

"You could've died!" Klarys exclaimed and she fought back tears. Her voice still broke with emotion. "You almost...you almost died...!"

"Y-yeah..." Mekial twisted to see that the guardsman's arrow had plunged into a tree several yards away.

It had been on a direct, collision course with him. Nothing could've stopped it.

So what did?

"The fires went out," Lilian observed, looking around. "They went out when you…" She broke off with a thick gulp.

At that she, Mekial and Klarys looked at the guardsman who'd been killed by his own sword. His only working eye was agape and his distorted face was further disfigured by the open-mouthed glower that it was frozen into.

Klarys vomited.

"Klarys!" Lilian went to her, one hand flying up to rub her back, and as the girl recovered she turned to see Mekial rise.

His could feel his whole body shaking. He wondered if anyone could see it.

"Mekial?" Lilian asked warily, concerned by his stiff expression. "How did…how did you do all of that?"

He didn't answer.

"D…do you think it's like Kro said?" Dillon tried. "That you're an innate?"

Mekial met Dillon's anxious look. But he still didn't answer.

He knew he'd kicked the first guardsman harder than he was normally capable of, and that he'd thrown the dagger at the other with an incredible amount of speed and dexterity, despite the fact that he wasn't used to its weight. Maybe he was learning a lot more in his training sessions than he'd originally thought. Or maybe it was the adrenaline.

Or was it really the aether?

For some reason, he couldn't bring himself to think about that being a possibility right now. His hands were trembling. His throat was dry. His heart was pounding.

He just wanted to go home.

"Let's get out of here," he said at last.

Dillon adjusted Kurt on his back and started to follow him. But at the sound of a light whimper, his stark green eyes dropped to Lacey.

She was trembling, her fearful eyes on the guardsman who had a knife sticking out of his head.

Dillon took her by the hand. "It's them or us, Lacey."

Startled, she looked up at him.

"Don't be scared," he said and he squeezed her hand gently. "We're all gonna make it outta here together."

She stared at him. Then, pressing her lips together, she nodded frightfully.

Keeping a strong hold on her hand, Dillon hustled after the others.

But once again, they found themselves running aimlessly. With no landmark or clear path to follow, they had no way of knowing which way led home and which way led to more imperials.

Their desperation dissolved into despair and shortly thereafter, Dillon began to slow down.

But it wasn't due to fatigue. With Kurt's face hanging beside his, he'd caught the dangerous change in his friend's breathing.

"Hey!" he called and the others turned as he knelt down and lay Kurt on the ground.

They gathered around the pair and their alarm peaked when they saw how weak Kurt looked. With his blonde eyebrows crinkled across his forehead he was breathing shallowly, one wheezing breath preceding another.

Fear thundered through their veins.

Dillon's heart rate spiked when he caught the sound of an approach. His head snapped up.

A trio of guardsmen had found them and after taking a short survey of the young villagers, the one in the middle spoke up. "Take the goblins to the camp," he said darkly. "As for the savages…" He gave Mckial, Klarys and the unconscious Kurt a once-over, likely pausing to consider their youth. He dismissed it. "We don't need them."

Silently his men advanced, hands going for their swords.

The children huddled nearer to one another.

Dillon leaned over Kurt protectively.

At the front of the group, Mekial dropped a hand to where his knives were and groped for their handles. But they weren't there.

It took him a split second to remember why. Even so, he widened his stance before his friends.

No sooner had he taken this position did a black-clad figure leap out from behind a tree near the commanding guardsman. A flash of silver showed that his sword was already drawn.

In the blink of an eye he was behind the imperial, one hand latching around his chin to expose his neck.

Flicking his blade out and over the vulnerable area, the warrior slashed his sword across it and flung the man's body away, then turned his masked face to the guardsmen who remained.

Overcoming their surprise, they launched at him with their swords out.

The warrior deflected their strikes, creating a clang of metal that sang a furious duet with the crackling forest. He was lithe, nimble, and despite the fact that he was facing elite members of the Empire's forces — outnumbered, no less — he held his own.

Blocking one of the guardsmen's attacks with an upward stroke, he cut across his neck with a second swing, killing him. Turning on the other, he struck him with a kick so ferocious that the man actually spiraled and smashed into a tree face-first. Without a sound, he sank against it.

The warrior turned on the children next. It was then they realized that he was wearing a mask.

With its horrible fangs drawn into a cheek-high grin, it seemed to be aware of some heinous punchline that no one else had heard, and a wild mane of hair framed its lion-like face. But its most prominent feature was on its brow.

Painted there was the Liberation Fronts' insignia of encircling and partly disconnected rings.

Mekial frowned.

Quaking with a fear that she desperately tried to hide, Klarys hid Lacey behind her.

Lilian inched behind Mekial.

Dillon continued to cover Kurt.

The man said nothing. It was like he was frozen as he watched them, studied them.

Then, with his bloody sword at his side, he marched towards them, his frightening face silhouetted against the flames that lashed in the distance.

Mekial's knees buckled in preparation of a fight, and he fought to find his voice. It shook out of his throat before he managed to even it out. "Leave us alone!"

The man stopped.

Mekial hid his shock and remained in that protective stance in front of his friends. He tried to sound strong in spite of the terror pounding through him. "Who are you?"

The swordsman didn't reply. The only thing he did was swipe his sword to the side, spattering the ground with gore. It was then that the children noticed the blade.

It was of Avat craftsmanship.

Mekial spoke up again. "Well?"

Crackling flames filled in for the man's silence. At long last, he replied.

"It's a long walk back to Taranis." His voice sounded just as sinister as his mask looked. "If you want to make it home, you'd better stick with me."

63

ROM THE EDGE of Taranis, Ivan scowled at the smoky horizon edging the vale. Though the border scouts had taken off on the saigas a while ago, he could still spot their tiny forms making a beeline for Odelwhite. He wondered how much worse the fires would be by the time they got there.

As for what had caused them in the first place, he could make an educated guess.

His face darkened, only to completely break when a sonic boom rattled the sky.

He whirled in alarm. At the same time, two silver objects blasted overhead and shot towards the enclosing mountains.

He blinked his bright eyes hard, expecting the hallucination to pass.

But it didn't and when his back was hit with an aftershock of wind, he could only believe that what he'd seen was real.

In their homes the villagers were just as shaken, with people ducking instinctively and covering their heads as the Skycrafts blasted over. The faces of others appeared in windows, and a new wave of fear rushed through the community.

Unaware of the fright that they'd caused, Brent and Aaron kept a steady foot atop their Skycrafts' accelerators. Soon Taranis was left far behind and far beneath them, and the world blurred into a steady rush of green as they continued to ascend. It wasn't until they'd risen higher than the foothills did they start to slow down, opting for control over the thrill of speed.

As she adjusted to this new velocity, Renée managed to control her uneasy stomach. She'd never gone anywhere by air after all and had been shot full of fear upon takeoff. To help it she pinned her eyes to the horizon, hoping that avoiding the distancing sight of solid ground would appease her.

But the swelling cloud of smoke was there and staring at it didn't make her feel safer. Actually, it made her feel worse. It looked as if they were flying straight into the arms of a monster — one that shrouded its scaly body in smoke and crackling fire.

She swallowed and suddenly became aware of how calm Brent felt in her arms. He probably wasn't scared.

Somehow, that helped her relax. But when the world darkened, forced into shadow as they neared the expanding haze, any sense of courage that he'd instilled in her died.

Brent rose still higher, seeking to get a bird's-eye view of the raging wildfire. When he had it, his scowl broke and he released the accelerator, leaving his Skycraft to cruise to an almost dumbstruck halt.

Renée sucked in a breath.

Aaron sailed to a stop not too far below them and voiced his bewilderment at a horrified murmur, "Oh, no…"

The forest, its vastness greatly displayed from their vantage point, was an endless sweep of trees that disappeared into the smoke's undulating depths. On any other day its breadth would have been a sight to behold, but no such awe could inspire them now.

For the entire region that existed just outside of Taranis' barrier was completely aflame.

Fire lashed through the canopy in a mad rush to devour and dangerous hues of red and orange lit the ground. Glowing embers gleamed through the burning foliage and skeletal trees stood black against them, their boughs crumbling. Smoke sat as bleak clouds at their roots, and grassy clearings that were already scorched were outlined in fire. Elsewhere, areas that had yet to be burned were slowly drowning in haze.

Brent's eyes shot from one charred area to another, hunting blindly for a break in the destruction.

There were only a few scattered clearings that seemed to be relatively safe. Other than that, the only places of refuge were on the far edges of the fire, in places it hadn't reached yet. The river, which cut through the middle of it all, was also clear but could only be spotted through breaks in the smoke.

"That's one big fire," he remarked quietly.

"Yeah," Aaron agreed, rising to fly alongside him. "Think the aetheriests'll use the river to put it out? Or whatever's left of it."

"Maybe. But they'll have to work fast. In the meantime, we've gotta find Mek and the others."

"We should try landing there." Renée pointed to an area outside of the flames.

After gauging its safety, Brent made to descend. But when he caught a strange flicker of light in the fires, he stopped.

His eyes narrowed suspiciously. "What is that?"

The others looked to find what he was talking about.

In one part of the blazing wreckage, ribbons of fire were swirling and arching together. White-hot flames flickered within the red and as the tendrils joined they bulged at the center, swelling the growing sphere to the size of a horse cart.

Aaron squinted at it. "What the…?"

The fireball hovered in place for a moment, flames whipping across its surface as its shape rounded out.

Then it blasted towards them, smashing through dead branches and skeletal pines with more force than a cannonball.

Their eyes bulging Brent and Aaron swung apart, leaving the flaming missile to shoot off into the sky with a screaming hiss.

Aaron looked back. "What was that?!"

"Nothing good." Brent turned to see where it'd gone, only to have his eyes grow in horror.

The fireball was falling back towards them, flames dancing behind it as it zeroed in on their location.

He jolted out of his trance. *"Scatter!"*

Tilting his handle, Aaron shot out of the way.

Stomping on his accelerator, Brent took off in the opposite

direction.

With a bellow, the fireball split in half and tore after them both.

Aaron didn't look back at the half that followed him. Instead, with his ears tracking its movement, he ordered for Liam to hang on and proceeded to zigzag through the air — breaking left, jerking right, circling back —

But the fireball mimicked his every turn as if it was tied to the Skycraft itself.

"Think I'm gonna be sick…" Liam gagged, covering his mouth.

"What do you mean you're gonna be sick?!" Aaron snapped.

Liam dry-heaved.

"Don't you dare —!" Aaron froze in the midst of glaring at him, caught by the sight of the nearing fireball. "Forget it, just swallow it and hang on tight!" Twisting his handle, he picked up speed and whipped back around.

The fireball screeched after them, railing on their backs with its heat as it closed in.

"I've got an idea!" Brent shouted at Renée and he swerved away from the fireball that hounded them. "Hold on!" Swinging his handle to the right, he stomped on his accelerator and rocketed towards Aaron.

Scrunching her eyes shut, Renée clung to him with all her might.

Aaron saw them coming and, tightening his grip on his handle, he increased his own speed.

All the while, the fireball that followed him closed in slowly.

He tried to go faster, but his heel had pushed the accelerator into the deck as far as it could go. Evidently, the Skycraft's speed had a limit.

He clenched his teeth and leaned forward, his body moving on instinct as if some part of him trusted that the shift could help.

Liam followed suit, both of his hands gripping Aaron's shoulders as his bangs lashed across his forehead. His silver eyes had shrunken to slits in the blinding light, and the heat raged against his skin with such intensity that it felt like he was being baked alive.

"What're you doing?!" he managed to shout when he was able to perceive two nearing silhouettes. While he couldn't see their faces in perfect detail, he could figure out who they were.

"Just trust me!" Aaron hollered.

Brent leaned forward as well, his eyes narrowing against the wind and oncoming heat, and he steeled himself for what was next. "Hang on, Ren…!"

She just whimpered, her eyes still squeezed shut.

Across from them, Liam ducked his head down.

Aaron yelled —

And just before he and Brent could collide, they thrust their handles forward and dove.

Unable to follow such a rapid change of direction the fireballs slammed into each other, creating a terrible explosion of wind and fire.

Far below them, Aaron and Brent yanked their handlebars back, forcing their Skycrafts to curve out of the dive. Slamming on their accelerators, they bolted into the sky and leveled out as the last of the fireballs disappeared.

Renée bowed her head into Brent's back and released a shaky sigh.[tv]

Brent grinned dangerously and he looked for Aaron. His eyes gleamed when he found him. "You guys good?"

"We're fine," Liam answered.

"Says the guy who nearly barfed," Aaron grunted.

Liam ignored him, his ears having already attuned themselves to something in the air.

Brent did the same, as did Aaron.

The air was quaking around them, troubled by a strange emergence of sound that swam through the atmosphere. It sounded similar to the Skycrafts' takeoff but it was coming from below and it was mounting in volume.

In short time the sound thickened, rising until it was practically upon them.

All at once, Liam was struck with panic. *"Get outta the way!"*

Startled by his urgency, Brent and Aaron shot apart.

No sooner had they done so did the space where they'd been hovering explode, creating such a devastating crash of wind, fire and smoke that their Skycrafts trembled and their ears popped.

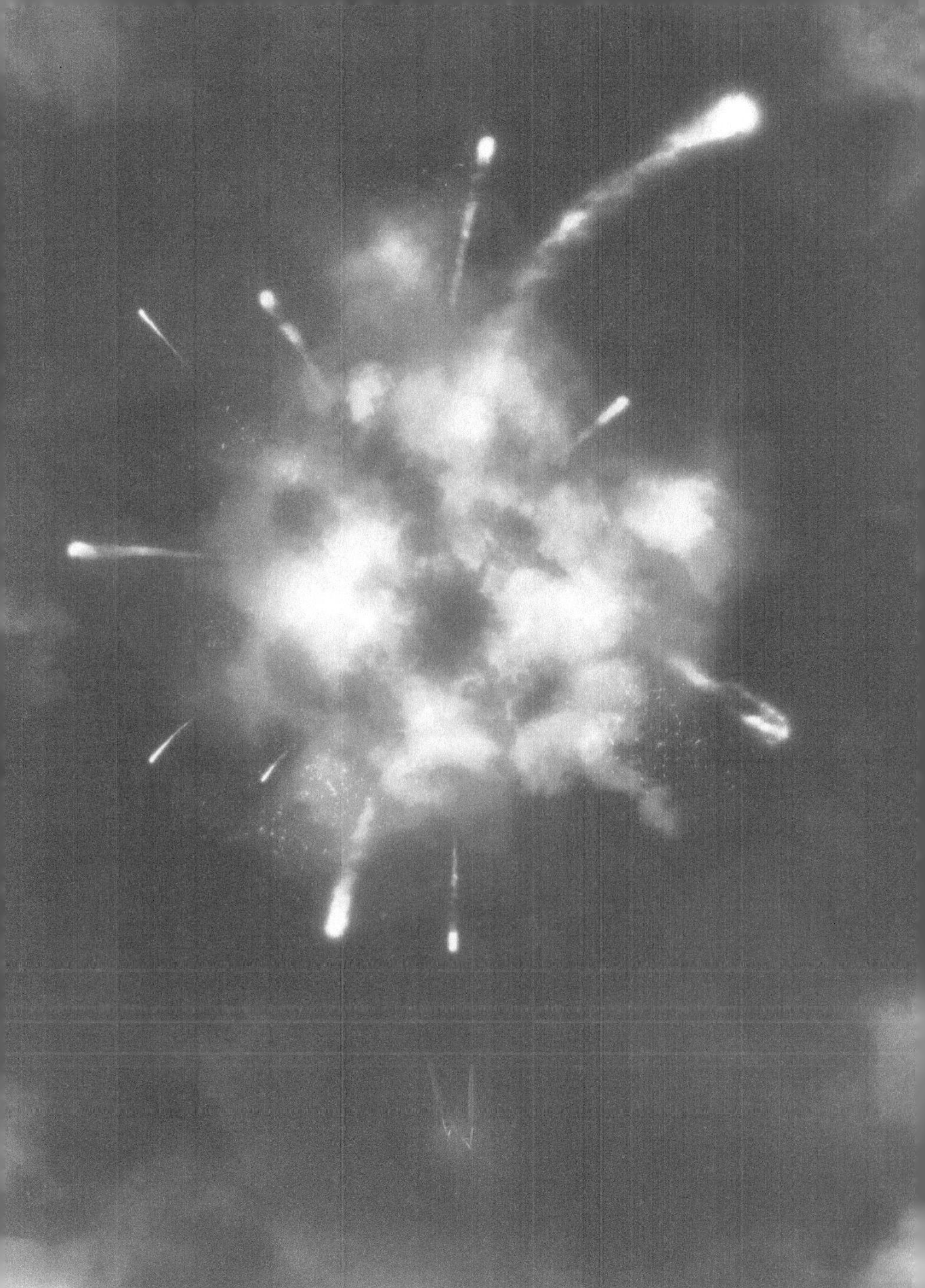

CAPTAIN REN
CODE: ACEPILOT

"Was that a bomb?!" Renée yelled but before any of her friends could answer the same storm of noise came again, this time swooping in from the left.

Without sparing a second they raced away and the space behind them was quickly rocked by another detonation.

"There's an opening below us!" Brent yelled at Aaron and the sound of another aerial explosion rumbled towards them. "This way! *Dive!*"

Tilting his craft, he streaked towards the ground with Aaron right behind him.

The air erupted at their backs once, twice, then again, each time buffeting them with hot gales that rocked their Skycrafts.

They didn't break course. But when an incoming eruption growled between them and their destination, they couldn't do it fast enough.

Just before the explosion, Brent tracked the noise to its source: it was a solitary figure, dressed in an armored collar, gauntlets and a purple and gold tunic — and he was standing in the fire. His hands were stretched towards the airborne group, palms glowing, skin glistening and yet, in spite of where he was, not a single part of him was aflame.

The vision of the guardsman was practically instantaneous, with Brent losing sight of him almost as soon as he saw him. At the same time his world shook, blinding light seared his eyes and with a deafening roar, wind and fire burst out of nothing to consume everything.

He and his friends were spared in the nick of time by a translucent wall that glimmered around them like solid crystal. It swallowed most of the explosion and deflected all of the fire, but the shock still sent them flying.

Thrown from their Skycrafts they crashed to the earth, each of them rolling in separate directions while their whirring vehicles skidded in another.

Grunting on impact, Brent rolled to a stop and clenched his teeth against the pain that gnawed at his skull. Water clouded his eyes in answer to the heat and as he blinked through it his ears rang, muting the voice of the flaming woods.

Wincing, he staggered to his feet and every bone in his body throbbed. It was a wonder nothing was broken.

All at once, his ears popped and the howling of the flames boomed around him. He squinted through the smog to get a good look at his surroundings.

There was a hilled path not too far away, marking the start of a towering wall of fire that stretched deep into the woods. What looked like the remains of a fallen tree wasn't too far from it, heaps of ash lying in place of its branches, and smoke was pooling at his feet like swamp water.

It all smelled horrible.

The air itself was choked with haze and drifting embers, setting the scene for an inferno that was on the brink of vomiting the damned. The last thing he wanted to do was linger.

He swiveled on the spot. "Ren?"

No one answered.

He spun again, his eyes darting between the oncoming flames and the shadows behind him. *"Renée!"*

"I'm here!"

Kicking into a run he followed the sound of her voice and found her inside of a shallow ditch, further from the flames. Dirt smeared her clothing as well as her face, but other than that she seemed all right.

Sliding down the incline, he offered a helping hand. "You okay?"

"Y-yeah…" She accepted his support. "I'm okay…"

He helped her out of the trench and when they reached its outer lip, they saw that Aaron and Liam were running to meet them. They were covered in soot and grime — Brent suspected that he looked just as terrible — but it seemed that at the very least neither of them had any serious injuries, either.

"You guys all right?" Aaron gasped.

"Yeah. Mostly." Renée leaned off of Brent when she'd gotten her bearings.

"Doubt we can fly the Skycrafts again," Liam said. "They don't look broken, but we might get caught in another explosion if we try to use 'em."

"The explosion…" Brent muttered, remembering, and he stepped towards the dancing fires, as if he expected a reappearance of the imperial who could walk through them.

"What?" Aaron picked up on his unease.

"I saw someone." Brent refaced all of them. "Right before that last explosion. He was standing in the fire and attacking us."

"Standing *in* the fire," Aaron repeated, thinking that Brent would reconsider his statement if he heard his own words spoken back to him.

"I know what I saw," Brent maintained and he looked at the smoking trees again. "He wasn't even burned…"

"An imperial?" Liam asked.

"Yeah." Brent called the image back to mind. "He had a crest on his front. He didn't look like a regular soldier, though. And he definitely wasn't a slave trader." He paused tensely, thinking. "I think… he was with Empyrean's Guard."

Renée's stomach twisted into an anxious knot.

Aaron's eyes hardened with suspicion and he turned on the fires. "Even if it was a guardsman, what kind of human being can stand directly in a fire and not go up in smoke? Not even an aetheriest could pull that off."

Brent's jaw clenched. He didn't have an answer.

"Whoever it is, and whatever they're capable of, we're too vulnerable our here in the open," Liam said plainly. "We got lucky by not crashing into the forest directly. We should keep moving."

"Speaking of, I wonder how we didn't blow up earlier," Renée added quietly.

"We got lucky," Liam said again. "Let's not push it."

"Right…"

Aaron's eyes fell from the woods to rest on the hazy ground.

Brent was the only one who noticed that he didn't appear to be completely present, as if he was analyzing several thoughts all at once.

"Oh." Aaron looked up sharply and turned to Renée. "Before I forget…" Reaching for something that was tucked into the back of his sash, he extended it to her. It was half of a hollowed out cylinder, scorched and disfigured. "I found this where me and Liam crashed. It looks like it's made up of the same material that the engineers use."

Renée took it from him to get a better look. "You think this is part of what Mekial and the others swiped from the workshop?"

"Can't say for sure. But it's definitely out of place here."

She looked up from the strange object worriedly.

"It's a lead." Brent's firm words caused Renée to look at him next. "Let's see where it takes us."

"Might have to wait." Liam's hand went for his sword. "We've got incoming."

Aaron faced the same direction as him and unholstered his tonfa. "Not like we would've gotten far anyway."

Brent took a step forward and listened.

Soon, he could hear it: the shrill clink of armor and the tromping of booted feet.

He reached for his bladed staffs.

Renée, her sword.

In seconds, the black outlines of four men crossed out of the fires and into the open.

Immediately Brent recognized their armor, with their purple tunics and armored collars, as well as the golden insignia that dominated their chests. It was the same as what the man standing in the fires had been wearing.

In all his time as an auction raider, Brent had never before crossed paths with a guardsman. Up until that moment, they'd only been the antagonists of differing reports that discussed the capture of sister villages.

But he remembered their descriptions, and knew of their imperial assignment to quell rebellions of any kind. Their presence was highly concentrated in the Province of Brusseir as of late, but that didn't mean they weren't active anywhere else.

And apparently, Taranis' activity as auction raiders had lead them to this southwestern corner of the continent, nearer to the largest Liberation Front that remained.

Brent didn't care how overwhelming their presence was, or how they were able to fight with fire the way that they could. All he knew was that as a slave auction raider of Taranis, he wasn't about to let them pass into the valley without a fight.

"It fell over here!" one of the guardsmen shouted to his allies and he turned, catching sight of the overturned Skycrafts in the process. Raising his eyes, he pinpointed their riders, who were already facing him with weapons bared.

His face opened. "Savages! Over here!" He drew his sword and unstrapped his shield from his back.

Brent, Aaron, Liam and Renée readied themselves.

Hardly a second later, Aaron felt a strange breath of air that led him to switch targets.

The guardsman at the group's rear was lifting a glowing hand.

Aaron opened his mouth to shout a warning to the others. But he just wound up gaping when, just as the aetheriest released a devastating blast, a clear barrier materialized around him. Trapped in the tiny space, the man's attack blew up in his own face, and plumes of smoke inhaled his body.

Without missing a beat, Renée and Liam rushed to face off against the first guardsman that had spotted them, she circling behind while he rushed at the man's front.

Blocking Renée with his shield and locking his sword against Liam's, the guardsman held his ground for the first few moments of battle. But the tides turned against him when Renée swept low, cutting at his calf and sending him to one knee.

Liam disarmed him and, snatching the man's sword out of the air for himself, he cut him down with both blades.

Renée spiraled, countering another imperial, and she made to strike him down.

But an arrow shot out of the darkness behind her and finished him off in her stead.

The only guardsman who remained was too engaged in his fight with Brent and Aaron to worry over the state of his comrades. But when the two suddenly jumped away from him, their sharp ears having tuned in to an odd rumble beneath their feet, he staggered, disoriented.

A second later, he was catapulted by a pillar of hard rock that jumped from beneath him. Crashing through branches, he sailed into the shifting smoke and out of sight with a fading scream.

Hearing a set of approaching feet, Liam turned to see who they belonged to. His friends followed suit, bracing themselves for another ambush. They dropped their stances when a pair of familiar faces emerged from the dark.

Brent's jaw dropped. "Aizen?!" he blurted, recognizing the giant intelligence scout as he neared them. His wide brow and auburn hair were telling, as was the scar that ran across his left eye. He was carrying a longbow and Brent quickly determined that the arrows from earlier had been his. His secondary weapon, a sickle, was belted to his side.

"Kyrah," Liam said, identifying the young woman that was with him.

"Liam?" The girl's face puckered with confusion.

"You guys're okay!" Brent exclaimed, his face brightening.

Kyrah didn't share his excitement. She seemed to be more taken aback than anything else. "Wha…?! What're you guys doing out here?! It's dangerous!"

"You first," Aaron replied. "Are all of the scouts from your rotation here, too?"

"Last I checked," Aizen responded, his heavy voice a perfect match for his muscular size.

"What happened to you guys?"

The scouts shared a short look with one another.

Aizen nodded his head to her silently.

"Empyrean's Guard got a lead on Taranis," Kyrah answered, staying her earlier surprise as she faced the raiders again. "They've been plotting this attack on Odelwhite for weeks, now. We managed to intercept them before they got here, so their numbers aren't nearly as high as they could've been. But that doesn't make things much easier, to be honest."

In a short second, Aaron understood. "That's why you guys ceased contact, isn't it? You didn't want Empyrean's Guard to find out where Taranis actually is."

Kyrah nodded to confirm. "The guardsmen have aetheriests, too, so we have to stay on our toes. As far as our numbers are concerned, well, we've only got one extra" — she shot a fast look at Aizen — "but if we work together, we should still be able to clear the imperials out."

"One extra?" Aaron frowned.

Liam didn't seem to care about that detail. "Reinforcements should be here soon, if they're not here already. Chief Ivan dispatched all of Taranis' aetheriests."

"Is that why you all are out here?" Aizen asked, hopeful. "Did the chief find out about the invasion and send forces to meet the guardsmen?"

"As much as we'd like that to be true, it's not." Aaron's eyes flicked in Renée's direction. "We're looking for Mekial, Lilian and some other kids from the village. Somehow, they got themselves out here before all of this got started."

Aizen frowned at that, troubled.

"We shouldn't waste anymore time then." Kyrah started to trek through the group. "This way. Aizen and I've already agreed to handle this area. The imperials are scattered and are wandering in small groups, but there might still be more around here."

"We'll have to be extra careful," Aizen informed the younger warriors. "These men aren't like any imperials we've fought."

"Yeah." Brent thought of the guardsman that he'd spotted in the fire. "We noticed."

"Keep close," Kyrah added, her pace rising to a jog.

The others picked up the pace, hurrying alongside her as they followed the line of fiery destruction deeper into the woods.

"Aw, that's kind of sad! They didn't even see that it was your barrier that saved them." As she spoke the young, dark-skinned woman cocked her head as if to feign disappointment. "Come to think of it, I don't even think that racist that you saved earlier knew that you helped him out, either."

Thin but fit, she wore a pair of tonfa on her hips whose blades were edged with black. A patterned band of cloth was bound to her small breast, decorated with white beads that gently clicked with her movements, and her low-waisted pants, loose at the bottom before cinching at mid-calf, elongated her bare midriff. A short, sleeveless vest was worn over her shoulders, clasped at the neck by a black brooch, and a silver bangle inlaid with shells hugged her wrists.

A half-mask hid her face, its features reminiscent of a calm lioness. Black with gold accents, the muzzle was shut and a long, sweeping ponytail hung from its crown to the small of her narrow back.

"Just goes to show that what the Elder says is a valid order," she continued, turning her hidden face to the man that she was addressing. He was crouching beside her on the thick bough that she herself was standing on. "We're only supposed to watch."

Oruviçu said nothing.

"But you're not a huge fan of that anymore, are you?" The woman leaned against the tree trunk nonchalantly. "Our Oruviçu, can't keep himself from saving a racist from being burned alive. Or from rescuing the descendant of a mass-murderer so he doesn't explode like he deserves. You're so strange."

"Viorë'to." Oruviçu didn't rise, didn't look at her. He only watched as Brent and the rest of his small party disappeared into the smog. "Can you hear him?"

The woman didn't reply, clearly confused.

"If you can't, then you should leave." Reaching up, Oruviçu removed his mask. His eyes, swirling with tones of teal, turquoise and gold, were a gateway to the cosmos. "Return to your duty… and I will begin mine."

Viorë'to started. "Wait a sec —"

"I'll see you on the island." He leaped to the ground.

When Viorë'to looked to see where he'd landed, she couldn't find him.

64

KRO AWOKE WITH a start.

He stared at the sky for a second, blinking weakly. Finally coming to his senses, he proceeded to pat himself down.

He wasn't dead.

He wasn't dead?

How was he not dead?

He sat up and held his head when it spun, hard. Pausing, he tried to remember what had happened.

He'd been with Mekial and the others, then Empyrean's Guard had showed up and had tried to capture the children…then there'd been an aetheriest who'd encased himself in flames before attacking Kro, blowing his shield to smithereens…after that, Kro had sent off a warning signal to Taranis before he'd completely blacked out.

Gripping his head harder, he shook it.

No, that's not right.

He was definitely forgetting something. But for the life of him, he couldn't remember what it was.

Funny how that worked.

Getting to his feet, he looked around.

He was standing at the crest of a foothill not far from the edge of the forest. Though shrouds of smoke drifted before his eyes, all but concealing the mountains and hills that walled off the valley, he could discern them well enough.

He turned around and his breath caught.

Odelwhite Forest was in flames, with lakes of fire burning through trees and underbrush as far as the eye could see.

He stared, hopeless and bewildered all at once.

"*Kro!*"

Hearing his name, he toppled out of his despair and hunted for the one who'd called him. Much to his surprise, it was Tyre.

Waving an arm at him, Tyre covered the last bit of distance between himself and his elder sibling.

Kro peeked beyond him: the other aetheriests of Taranis weren't far behind, each of them dismounting the saigas that they'd ridden all the way from the village.

"Am I glad to see you!" Tyre stopped in front of him, earning his brother's attention. "What happened? Are any of the other border scouts with you? You, Leigha, and Torrence were all on duty, right?"

Kro opened and closed his mouth. Finally, his brow crinkled sadly.

Tyre's face slowly morphed into one of horror.

"Kro."

The two circled around and saw that the coordinator of Taranis' aetheriests, Heldar, was hiking up the hill to join them.

Dressed in embroidered bottoms accented with beads, tassels, and a long train of printed cloth that reached for his ankles, Heldar was close in age to the village leader. His hair, straight and dark and barely brushing his shoulders, was held back with the help of a patterned headband, and its two tails hung beside his left ear. Across his left eye, there existed a long and jagged scar, though he wasn't blinded by it.

He stopped before them, eyes on Kro. "You sent up the warning signal?"

"Yes, sir." Kro hastily stood in an attentive position.

"Status."

"Sir. Empyrean's Guard has invaded Odelwhite Forest."

"They did this?" Heldar looked out into the flames, his bitter frown waning.

"Sir." As the other aetheriests joined their party, Kro kept his eyes on their coordinator. "And, well, this might sound crazy, but please believe what I'm about to say."

"And what's that?" Heldar faced him.

"I don't know how they're doing it," Kro's face was serious, "but Empyrean's Guard is using element armigers."

The way back to Taranis was riddled with guardsmen, some of whom Mekial and the others could spot from afar while others came running out of the ember-filled darkness with their weapons raised.

But each time they were ambushed, the masked swordsman took the attackers down with ease. He was formidable and ruthless in his offense, piercing his attacks with feigned motions and merciless strikes that hacked through his enemies' defenses. All through their escape, he left a trail of bodies in his wake.

His youthful followers did well to stay out of the way during his fights. But when Mekial spotted a guardsman raising his crossbow to strike him from behind, he couldn't stand back.

Running at the bowman on impulse, he rammed his shoulder into him and actually managed to knock him clean off his feet. As he fell, the boy robbed him of the sword on his belt and held it over his head to slay him.

But he froze, petrified by the sudden look of terror that had overtaken the imperial's young face.

The imperial shuddered, waiting for the final blow to come. But when he saw that Mekial wouldn't kill him, he aimed his crossbow at him and moved his finger to the trigger.

Mekial's entire body locked up, his eyes widening as the guardsman's narrowed with rage.

A curved sword came out of nowhere and struck the man where he lay.

Startled, Mekial stumbled back and lowered the imperial's sword to see who'd saved him.

"Kill or be killed," the masked warrior said plainly. "If you don't mean to assist, then don't get in the way."

Mekial stared at him, his mouth open, and he let his eyes fall to the imperial.

He wasn't sure why he'd stopped. Perhaps there was something different about killing someone for the sake of self-defense and killing someone who looked so scared.

"These men will take your life without hesitation," the swordsman continued, as if he could read the boy's thoughts. "Then they'll take the lives of your friends. Your family. Until you have nothing left."

At that Mekial looked at his friends, with their grimy faces and ripped clothing. They were watching him and the swordsman from the path.

He turned away. "…He looked scared," he said after a moment.

"Not when he was about to kill you." The swordsman bore no empathy for the boy. "I'd say you were the one who looked scared."

Mekial didn't respond.

The swordsman said nothing else. But he nodded to the other children as an indication and hurried along the road again.

"Mekial," Klarys called when she saw that he wasn't coming.

He circled to face her, his face pulled into a bothered frown. Then, clenching his new sword, he ran to catch up with her and everyone else.

He hardly noticed that the blade that he'd taken, forged with heavy metals and once owned by a full-grown man, was as light as a feather in his grip.

"Who do you think that man is?" Lilian asked the others, scurrying to keep up with their longer strides.

"I don't know," Klarys replied, "but his mask gives me the creeps."

"It's scary," Lacey agreed meekly.

"It doesn't matter who he is," Dillon said objectively. "We're a lot better off with him than we are without him."

"I don't think we should trust him," Klarys said.

"I don't even know if I do," Dillon admittedly thoughtfully, glancing down, "but, if he can get us back to Taranis, I'm okay with him. For Kurt's sake."

His friends agreed silently.

It wasn't long before they came across another small party of imperials.

This time, Mekial didn't hesitate.

Joining with the masked warrior's advance, he moved in to help defeat the invaders. He took advantage of any opening he could get, be it when a soldier's foot suddenly got caught in a gnarled bush or sank into a random hole; one was even struck with a falling branch, and another tripped over a lump in the earth.

With the flat side of his sword Mekial battered them unconscious, his arms helped by a surge of strength that no one would've thought him capable of. Indeed, fighting him was like fighting two opponents at once: untimely jinxes and a full-fledged fighter trapped in a boy's body.

He was still scared. But what scared him more was being unable to protect those he cared about.

None of his friends could defend themselves and Jeffrey, one of the village's strongest, was training him to aid in Taranis' battle against the Empire. He refused to stand by and let it all go to waste, especially considering what Renée had done so that he could continue his training. If this was what he was being prepared for, then he'd throw himself at it with all he had.

If this was what it took to save those he loved, then he'd fight with all his strength.

Somewhere behind him Lacey screamed frightfully, overwhelmed by the bloodshed when the battle was over. As Mekial and the swordsman ran ahead, Dillon seized her by the hand.

"C'mon, Lace!" he shouted over her shrieking. "We have to keep going!"

Her cries lowered, her breath escaping her as teary-eyed gasps. Swallowing her terror, she went with him.

But she couldn't tear her eyes away from the carnage.

"Just look at me!" Dillon told her and he squeezed her tiny fingers. "Look at us!"

Hair lashing and her feet skittering to keep up with his, she did just that.

"Take her, Klarys!" Dillon shouted to her, giving her Lacey's hand, and when Klarys took it he readjusted Kurt on his back.

"It's gonna be okay, Lacey!" Klarys said to her. "Just hang on!"

Lacey whimpered, tears spilling down her cheeks.

In the middle of the group, Lilian scurried to keep pace with everyone. Eyes scrunching and lips curling, she cried silently.

Stolen sword still in hand, Mekial sprinted at the front of their party and did well to keep his eyes on the road ahead. He skidded to a stop when another pair of guardsman were spotted but before he could even offer his aid, the stranger finished them off and waved the children forward.

Mekial went first. He couldn't stop himself from glancing at the ruined bodies of the soldiers that the swordsman had just defeated.

His stomach flipped.

He'd been taking out his opponents with rather pointed strikes, opting to knock them out instead of outright kill them. But the injuries that the nameless warrior had given to these men…it looked like slaughter.

His hands tightened around the hilt of his weapon and his stomach sank with dread.

Was that how he was supposed to be handling his enemies? Kill them without thought? Was that really what this battle called for?

Was this really what he was being trained for?

It seemed he'd been romanticizing the idea of becoming an auction raider. Did Brent, Aaron and Liam face this much bloodshed when they rescued slaves? What about his father? And his mother?

He bit hit lip.

He couldn't dwell on issues of morality now. They had to survive this ordeal first.

"Look out!" Lilian suddenly yelled, and Mekial was torn from his thoughts.

A guardsman was standing at the rise of the next hill. With a wave of his arm, he caused the ground to vomit a surge of stalagmites that rushed towards the group — rushed towards the swordsman.

"NO!" Mekial yelled and he cast out his hand, as if that could stop the rocks.

But it couldn't. So the pillars of stone continued to surge out of the earth, closing in on the children's savior with the aim of impaling him. Their speed was impeccable. No man, however agile, could even think to avoid them.

Behind his mask, the warrior's blue eyes grew large.

Suddenly, light blinked right in front of him. Then, solidifying into one shining point of illumination, it swallowed the area in a glare so magnificent that it was blinding.

The children turned away.

When the light finally faded, the swordsman saw that a transparent wall was arcing over him, sparkling like starlight.

All at once the torrent of moving rock smashed into it, sending broken bits of stone flying everywhere.

Dillon, Klarys, Lacey and Lilian gawked at the barrier, their eyes reflecting its shimmering form. When it suddenly shattered of its own accord they flinched, then watched in amazement as its broken body sprinkled the air with what looked like cosmic dust.

Flourishing his sword in the midst of this glittering rain, the masked stranger darted around the smashed bulges of rock and closed in on the guardsman, who raised his hand again to exact another aetherial strike.

But the swordsman swung beneath his wrist and thrust his blade through the man's torso.

The aetheriest gagged and choked, startled by the suddenness of the attack. As his body dropped, the swordsman turned on Mekial.

The boy wasn't looking at him. Instead his wide, brown eyes were fixed on his extended hand, from which a powerful light was fading from his palm. At the same time he could feel a foreign presence pulling away from him, its invisible fingers peeling off of his as it retreated into the shadows, into the intangible currents of the air.

Klarys' mouth dropped. "Mekial! Did you just —?!"

"Whoa," Dillon breathed.

Lilian stared, teary-eyed.

Lacey did the same, drops of water clinging to her eyelashes.

Though his eyes couldn't be seen, Mekial could feel the swordsman's hard gaze lingering on him. He didn't meet his stare until the light in his hand completely died.

The stranger studied the boy's sword for a second. "…Now I get it."

Mekial stared at him.

"You're no ordinary fighter, are you boy?"

"I…well, I…" Mekial puckered his brow and remembered that the swordsman was bringing them back to Taranis. That had to mean he was at least a supporter, right? "I'm in…auction raid training…"

"Auction raid?" He could almost hear the man smiling. "Are they training aetheriests to fight like raiders, now?"

Mekial and his friends froze, not sure whether they'd heard him correctly.

"I guess it would catch the Empire off guard…and it explains the way you've been fighting up until now." The swordsman noticed Mekial's dumbfounded expression. "You really didn't know."

Mekial just gaped at him and then at his hand.

He was an aetheriest.

He was an *aetheriest!*

He suddenly remembered the abrupt sting of cold that had materialized back when he and the others had been trapped in fire. Then he looked at his sword and for the first time noticed its size. Now that he thought about it, it was strange that he was able to swing it around so easily. Was the aether helping him with that, too?

Suddenly, all of the unexplainable things that he'd been able to do up until that point made sense and he felt stupid for not accepting it sooner.

Kro had been right. He was an aetheriest.

And not just any aetheriest — he was an *innate.*

Pride swelled in his chest, only to peter out rather quickly.

He wasn't entirely fond of Kro. He thought he was weird because he often tried flirting with his sister. But, that didn't change the fact that he wished Kro could've seen what he'd just done.

He wondered if he was all right.

The swordsman grew weary of his silence. "It doesn't matter. I'm not one for children fighting my battles, but I won't complain if you decide to cover me again."

Looking up, Mekial just nodded wordlessly.

"But that's all you should do." The swordsman seemed to fix him with an icy stare, one that made his mask that much more chilling. "You've been giving us a good advantage, but I'm tired of cleaning up after you. If you're going to face an imperial, kill him on the spot. Don't waste time by giving him the chance to live with the knowledge that the so-called 'savages' the Empire hunts are living near this forest."

Mekial stiffened, his stomach lurching.

"This way." Continuing over the hill, the man vanished over its crest.

Mekial hesitated. Then, he hurried after him.

"Wow, Mekial," Dillon said, coming up beside him. "You're seriously an aetheriest!"

As if that alone confirmed what he'd been hoping to be true for such a long time, joy returned to Mekial's eyes. For a moment, he forgot the swordsman's chastisement. "Yeah!" He beamed. "Toldja!"

Klarys rolled her eyes.

Mekial saw her. "Aw, c'mon Klarys, gimme some credit! That barrier was pretty cool, huh?"

Klarys didn't feed his ego. She looked at Dillon. "How's Kurt?"

"He doesn't sound as bad," he informed her as their friend bounced against his shoulders. "But the sooner we can get him to Khirsta, the better."

"Hang in there, Kurt," Lilian said, touching the boy's hand as she ran.

Mekial slid their sleeping friend a troubled look before facing forward again. Once more, his mind returned to the swordsman.

How could he tell so easily that he was an aetheriest? And how did he know about auction raid training and Taranis? Was he really a supporter like he'd thought earlier? Were there more in the woods right now? Or perhaps there were other people from Taranis?

He had so many questions. But given the circumstance, he couldn't ask them now.

He could worry about it all when they finally made it home.

65

AIZEN LOOSED AN arrow, stunning a guardsman right before he could strike Renée.

Seizing the opening, she slashed the imperial's face.

He collapsed with little more than a grunt.

At her back, Brent clobbered another guardsman with the knobbed ends of his staff. Spinning his weapon, he unsheathed its swords and struck him down.

Straightening, he cleaned his blades with a hard swipe of them across the air. He lifted his head. "That fire's getting closer," he said.

With their allies fighting behind them, Renée followed his gaze.

They'd been doing their best to travel at a safe distance along the burning forest's edge while searching for Mekial and his friends. But it already looked like the flames had closed more than half that space. Even now the air was thicker, and Renée could feel the heat stinging her eyes.

She took a step back. But then she noticed something: the flames were moving in a perfectly straight line. There was no break in their uniformity, no dissonance in their approach. They were like nature's answer to a line infantry.

"Is it me…" she turned to Brent, "or are those fires coming at us like a wall? It's like they're…controlled."

Brent's eyes narrowed and he considered her description. *Controlled.*

Glancing up, Renée watched as the smoke that billowed out of the flames joined the swirling abyss in the sky. Somewhere in the smog, the sun hovered as a crimson circle.

She turned to Brent again. This time, there was fear in her eyes. "Brent, what if…what if we don't find them?"

He scowled, more so at the hopeless idea than at her. "Ren, we're gonna —"

Something exploded, shaking the air and the ground with a cataclysmic *bang!*

She and Brent flinched, as did the others, who'd just finished clearing out the other guardsmen.

Renée righted herself. "What was —?!"

She turned on the fires, as did Brent.

Directly in front of them a fireball was curling out of the flames, its body swirling into existence just like the one that had nearly blown them out of the sky earlier. It swelled quickly, taking on the size of a miniature sun in a matter of seconds.

Renée gaped, dumbstruck.

Brent's eyes were large. "Uh…uh-oh."

With ribbons of fire crossing it like solar flares, the fireball screamed towards them.

"Look out!" Pulling Renée into his chest, Brent turned his back on the missile and held on to her.

Light flickered behind him and he braced himself.

But the impact never came. The light only got brighter, stretching his and Renée's shadows across the land.

Then the shine itself solidified, hardening into a soaring dome that curved around them and the rest of their group.

The fireball detonated against it, spitting wind and flame in every direction. Trees were blasted out of the ground and cinders spun everywhere; the smoke dispersed with a roar and overhead, the black clouds rippled.

When it was over, the aetherial barrier dissolved into glittering dust.

Still holding Renée, Brent lifted his head to look around.

Renée peeked out along with him.

Lowering his arms, Aaron glanced around before noticing Kyrah. "Nice reflexes," he said.

She shook her head. "That wasn't me."

He frowned.

"You guys might wanna hit the dirt!"

Recognizing the voice, Aaron and the others looked up to see Tyre and Kro racing into view.

Farther away, another ball of flame came into being and screamed towards them.

Tyre ran to a spot in front of everyone. As the fireball closed in, he stretched one hand forward and spun his wrist.

Wind circled in front of him, swirling into a horizontal tunnel that grew to hurricane-like strength.

With a deafening bellow, the fireball crashed into this wind and ruptured, its center expanding as the whirlwind drilled through it. The dispersing flames spiraled outward like a windmill.

Spreading her feet, Kyrah erected a shield around the party. Like every other quintessent wall that had been built thus far, it deflected the fireball's explosion.

Kro caught up with his brother, one hand latched around his opposite bicep. Electricity danced between his finges.

When Kyrah's shield disintegrated, he thrust his crackling arm forward and unleashed a wide-ranged blast of light.

Tyre and everyone else turned away to protect their eyes. At the same time, a large stretch of the fires blew out.

Standing in their place was a guardsman, his hands glued to his eyes as he stumbled backward, screaming.

Brent stared at him, wide-eyed.

While he'd been sure that he'd already seen a guardsman standing in the fires, there was something different about witnessing proof of it so clearly.

Hardly affected by the imperial's reveal, Tyre traced a circle around him in midair with one hand and punched with the other, firing a beam of energy that nailed him right in the head.

With the palest of grunts, the man collapsed. He didn't move again.

"All right!" Kro faced Tyre triumphantly. "Way to go, little bro!"

"We're on a roll!" Tyre grinned and high-five'd him. "It's a good thing we brought some of Khirsta's elixirs with us. You'd probably be out of the aether for days, otherwise!"

Something moved in the corner of his vision and when he looked to see what it was, he learned that the others were drawing near.

Liam took the liberty of addressing the aetheriests first. "We owe you one," he said.

"It's what we're here for!" Tyre returned with a broad smile. It quickly faded. "Wow. You guys look awful."

"We're not exactly skipping through daisies," Aaron snipped.

At that point, Kro spotted the older villagers. "Kyrah?" He gaped. "Aizen! Wait, so are all the scouts here?"

"Yeah," Brent replied and he filled them in on what had been keeping the scouts from Taranis.

"Right." Kro remembered the interaction he'd had with the guardsmen before the chaos had begun. "The Guard doesn't know exactly where Taranis is. They only know that we're somewhere near Odelwhite. But, given all that's going on, that's not exactly encouraging."

"What's your status?"

"It's not as straightforward as we would've hoped," Tyre began. "The fires aren't exactly…normal."

"What's that mean?"

"They're…" Tyre looked like he didn't want to say the answer for fear of not being believed.

"I was out here on patrol earlier, so I know how it started," Kro said, coming forward. "The aetheriests in Empyrean's Guard are using element armigers. They're literally encasing their bodies in fire and fighting us with it. There's a whole line of them, marching across Odelwhite and burning everything in their path. Right now, whole segments of that wall of fire are being controlled by a different imperial."

Brent and Renée exchanged looks.

"Armigers," Aaron echoed, his icy blue eyes narrowed in thought. "Like from the stories? And our schoolhouse plays?"

Tyre cast Kro a worried glance and nodded.

Aizen and Kyrah made a similar exchange, though theirs was more morbid than anything else.

At first, Aaron appeared to be disbelieving. Then, his eyes brightened with remembrance and he turned aside sharply. He cursed under his breath.

Before Kro could question him, Liam came forward. "You said you were out here on patrol. Did you happen to see Lilian out here?"

Tyre's eyes stretched to the size of saucers. "Your *niece* is out here?!" he shouted, pointing at the ground to indicate the flaming forest. "Why?!"

"We don't know yet," Renée said and she went on to explain why she, Brent, Liam and Aaron had ventured to the woods at all. She mentioned Harver's invention when the brothers inquired as to how they'd arrived without mounts of their own — though she didn't dive into any details about how it worked — and concluded with how they'd run into Kyrah and Aizen.

When she finished, Kro was stiff and tight-lipped.

"You really didn't see Mekial or any of them?" she asked.

"Sorry, Ren." Tyre was remorseful. "I would've told you if I had. I didn't even know our scouts weren't missing anymore until just now." He looked at Aizen and Kyrah indicatively.

Kro kept his mouth shut.

Renée's face saddened.

"We're gonna find them, Ren," Brent promised. "Don't worry."

His confident assurance stirred something within her, for she hopefully lifted her head a little.

Kro glanced between them, envious and guilty all at once.

Another *bang* snapped across the smoldering clearing, and a wave of fire leaped up in place of the one that had been extinguished.

"What the heck?!" Tyre exclaimed.

"Don't tell me he got back up," Kro groaned.

A shrill whistle pierced the sky, and they all looked up.

Another fireball was swooping towards them, nose-diving to set them alight.

"Look out!" Lifting her hands, Kyrah started to forge another barrier.

Tyre assisted.

Their shield barely materialized before the fireball crashed into it, and the resulting explosion sent them all flying.

Rolling to a stop, Tyre flipped onto his back with a loud and painful gasp. He sounded like he'd just emerged from underwater.

Several yards away Kyrah did the same, every end of her body tingling.

"Tyre!" Having landed near him, Kro commando-crawled to his brother, who could only cough and gasp in response. "C'mon, breathe, buddy!"

Tyre kept gasping. At last he managed to regulate his airflow, but he continued to cough sporadically. His body jerked with each expulsion of air, every part of him fighting to stabilize itself.

"That's it, man, c'mon," Kro encouraged. "You just got knocked outta the aether, you're good!"

Tyre nodded weakly, still coughing, his chest still heaving.

Kro fought off panic.

Tyre didn't look good.

"I'm…okay…" Kyrah huffed when Aaron showed up beside her, his bright eyes lit with concern. "Just got…caught off guard…"

"Incoming!" Brent yelled from elsewhere.

Kro looked up, and his olive eyes grew at the sight of another fireball arching towards them from across the field.

Cursing, he scrambled to his feet. With Kyrah and Tyre down, he was the only one capable of protecting everyone.

No pressure, he told himself.

Running straight for the ground-based meteor, he stretched one hand towards a pile of fallen trees that were lying just beyond him.

They shifted slightly. Then, gathering together, they followed the turn of his hand and blocked the fireball's path.

The ensuing collision knocked him clean off his feet. He rolled through the air before landing in a heap near his brother, and remnants of the shattered trees flew over him to vanish into the smoke.

"Okay," he grimaced as Tyre carefully rolled onto his stomach next to him. "That hurt a lot."

Collecting himself, Tyre looked up in time to see that the rest of their party was gaining the strength to stand.

He tried to do the same, but it felt like an entelodon was sitting on his back. It was all he could do to keep himself propped on his elbows.

Panting, Renée swept the area with her eyes.

All around them a new enclosure of flames danced, lashing much closer to them than ever before. The air was thick with ember-filled smoke, heat stifled their breath, and sweat soaked their clothes. If nothing was done soon, they'd be roasted alive.

"There's…no way out…" she puffed weakly.

Brent was equally winded, for the air quality was low thanks to the fires. He flicked his gaze up when a new storm of heat crashed into them.

Three fireballs were hovering close to their gathering now, and all of them were at least twice the size of the ones that had appeared previously.

He squinted in their light.

"Huddle!" Aizen called out and everyone complied, with Aaron, Renée and Aizen himself helping one aetheriest each.

Hardly a second later the hovering fireballs changed shape: stretching themselves into towering walls, they penned the group in on all sides.

A familiar pressure brushed against them at the same time, and a short glance around showed that Kyrah had evidently reconnected to the aether: her hands were stretched, palms were alight and a barrier was separating them from the nearing flames.

But, given its thinness, it was evident that she was still recovering from the last attack.

"Kyrah…don't…" Tyre tried, meaning to warn her of what overexertion could do to her body. But he couldn't finish, and had to lean on Renée for support.

Pushing himself off of Aizen, Kro threw his hands up and reinforced Kyrah's shield with another.

His head spun wildly and his knees buckled to sustain him.

Digging his feet into the ground, he forced himself to at least hold that stance. If he could just do that, the barrier wouldn't fall.

He couldn't let it fall.

"Any ideas?" Liam asked, looking to Brent out of the side of his eye.

"If we had one more aetheriest we could go underground," Brent answered distractedly.

They were stuck. Two aetheriests were trying to keep their shields up while the third was incapacitated. If just one of them tried to do something else — anything else — they'd be cooked.

Literally.

He clenched his teeth.

It couldn't end here. It couldn't.

He blinked, startled.

Someone was standing just beyond the barriers, not far from the flames. He bore no weapons, and had no means of defending himself.

What was more, he'd appeared out of nowhere.

The others saw him, too.

"Who's that?" Aaron asked, voicing everyone's thoughts.

Although his back was to them Brent soon recognized him, for he placed the figure's dark silhouette and mane of wild hair at Renée's graduation, upon the hill of Taranis' main road.

But…why was he here again now?

All at once a heavy, pressurized force struck them, birthing itself from the stranger's position.

It was his quintessence, they realized, but its weight was far more than anything they'd ever felt. It enriched the ashy air, making their skin crawl, and it hung over them like a refreshing wind amidst the heat that strangled their lungs.

Overwhelmed, Kyrah and Kro dropped their barriers. Stumbling backward, they altogether staggered out of their own connection to the aether.

Before them, a circulating wind enclosed their rescuer. Faster and faster it spun, growing to surround the villagers at the same time, and as it expanded a pale green light bloomed in the stranger's face.

The entire world seemed to go silent in that moment, with every crackle, every groan of fire fading into nothing. The light increased at the same time, washing away all other color, all other shapes and silhouettes until there was nothing left —

Brent blocked his eyes with his arms. And though there was

no wind his hair and clothes continued to shake; though there was nothing around him, he felt like he was surrounded by everything.

He chanced to lower his arms and squinted at his surroundings.

Turquoise and gold mist was swirling all around him, with shallow waters of glass at his feet and open skies banding over his head.

He glanced about, confused, for none of his friends were with him anymore, and the wildfires of Odelwhite weren't even pinpricks on the horizon.

But then he circled, and learned that he wasn't truly alone: for, where the masked figure had once been standing, there was now someone else.

It was a man, that same one with ornamented clothes of white and a high-drawn ponytail that undulated in a humming gust. It billowed towards his ankles, and the ends of his pointy ears were visible in the mist. The feathered ring that pierced one of them tinkled softly.

As if he could sense Brent's gaze, or perhaps even his presence, the man began to turn.

"You were told. Remember?"

Brent glimpsed a pair of narrow, golden eyes and a face of light brown skin. But the rest of the man's features were completely out of focus.

"I know it looks bad. But there's something else for you to do. So you can't fall here."

Brent blinked and a storm of images struck him: a blue-haired Avat boy crying, alone; that same boy, now a man, using his body as a barrier to protect a group of people from a danger that Brent couldn't see; that same man standing in the middle of a wasteland, his hair lashing, eyes crackling with lightning; a scaly, horned beast whose webbed wings stretched into the sky —

"You have to go back. But don't forget."

— an antlered black lion with fangs bared and eyes of white —

"Çaru'qu doesn't make mistakes."

The light cleared, softened. Died.

Brent shaded his eyes with an arm again, allowing himself to readjust to the dimming scenery. When it seemed safe to look around, he did so.

All of the fire was gone.

And there were three guardsmen lying on the ground now, unmoving.

"What the…" Aaron chanced a few steps forward.

"It's all gone."

Heads turned to Tyre, who was staring out over the rest of the woods.

Everyone else looked around.

He was right. There wasn't a flame in sight. Moreover, between the skeletal remains of trees and swampy bushes, the distant corpses of guardsmen were visible.

A drop of water hit Brent's nose. He looked up.

Rain descended.

66

"WHO WAS THAT?" Renée scanned the area. But there was no sign of the masked man who'd saved them. "And how did he clear everything out so fast?"

"No idea," Liam responded quietly, his wet hair already clinging to his face.

"Even the guardsmen…" Aaron didn't continue. Rather, his frown deepened.

Brent stared into the rainstorm vacantly, his blue hair plastered to his forehead. The strange words that he'd now heard twice continued to play in his ears:

Çaru'qu doesn't make mistakes.

"Tyre. Kyrah." Kro turned to look at the two, one arm wrapped around his side. "We should try to meet up with the aetheriests. Make sure everything's really safe."

"You shouldn't push yourself," Renée said, coming towards him. She caught him when he nearly stumbled in place. "You need to rest somewhere dry."

Kro's eyes, tight with pain, rested on her concerned face for a second. Standing, he stepped away from her. "I'll be fine." He turned to Kyrah and his brother. "We can take the saigas back."

"You're right," Kyrah agreed. "Let's go. C'mon, Tyre." Helping the younger brother along, the two followed after Kro.

"I'll rendezvous with the other scouts," Aizen said, his grey eyes moving to Renée through his long, rain-plastered hair. "I'll keep a lookout for Mekial and the others."

"Thank you," she said.

Liam nodded stiffly.

And so, Aizen separated from them as well.

"Brent?" Renée looked at him, noticing that he was still staring into space.

He faced her wordlessly.

"Are you okay?"

"I…" He shook his head and a hand absently went to his sky blue hair. "Yeah. I'm fine."

Renée didn't appear to be convinced, but she didn't press the matter.

Aaron flipped wet bangs out of his face and squinted through the sheets of rain. Then, turning in the muck that was quickly swamping his animal-hide shoes, he offered a change of pace:

"We're gonna need to split up if we wanna keep looking for Mekial and his friends," he said through the shower. "We'll cover more ground that way. Besides, there's still a chance there's some guardsmen hanging around. Last thing we need is for them to find the kids first."

"We should check the area south of the river then," Brent seconded. "They might've stayed near it."

"Wait." Liam held up a hand, his ears prickling as he listened through the sigh of rain.

His friends watched him.

Liam didn't move and behind his limp bangs his irises trembled, something that the others had learned was more noticeable whenever he was focusing on something that his eyes couldn't register.

At last, he heard it again: a tiny voice that hailed him from afar. *"Uncleee!"*

He spiraled. "Lil?!"

The others whirled as well, listening.

In a matter of seconds a small being came running at them from a distance, her small face splattered with mud as she hurried through the wet terrain.

Liam didn't recognize her at first, but her gait soon did well to tell him who she was.

"Lilian!" Relief swept through him and he made to go to her. He only took a step before another sound burst into his ears.

Convinced of its threat, he drew his sword with a raging glare and ran to meet it.

The guardsman came stumbling out of the wet trees a moment later, his uniform in tatters and his body riddled with wounds that were still bleeding.

Lilian skittered to a slippery stop, her dirty face opening in terror at the sight of him. Spinning around she tried to run away, but the imperial caught up to her in two strides and snatched her by the collar of her shawl.

She shrieked.

The guardsman cackled. "Thought you could get away, gob —?"

Spiraling into him, Liam hacked his arm clean off.

Screaming in shock, the man backpedaled.

Lilian crumpled into the mud.

Pivoting, Liam swung his foot into the guardsman's jaw, sending him flying into the nearest tree with the pop of bone and bark breaking.

He was dead before he hit the ground, muddy water spraying the air upon his impact.

Liam stood over his corpse in silence, his breathing quiet. Slowly, the fury that blazed in his light eyes melted away and when Lilian whimpered behind him, it vanished altogether.

Hastily, he put away his sword and went to her. "Lil? Are you okay?"

She looked at him tearfully. Her entire face seemed to have a spasm when he knelt before her. Scrunching her eyes shut, she threw her arms around his neck and held on tight.

Behind them Aaron suddenly spun about, his hands flying for his tonfa, and he raised them — blades out — just in time to guard against the sword of a man clothed in black. His arms bulged with the strain of keeping his attacker at bay and his bright eyes flashed at the man's ferocious mask.

Renée drew her sword, ready to assist, and while keeping Lilian back with one arm Liam twisted at the hip and grabbed the hilt of

SARUKE'S SHADE
CODE: VIGILANTE

his own blade.

Brent whipped his staff into a stance of battle, only to freeze when he recognized the stranger's mask.

It was the exact same one that he'd witnessed recently, from its mane of hair to the symbol of the Liberation Fronts painted across its forehead.

Yet, at the same time, there was something different about it.

Or, to be more precise, there was something different about the essence of the man who wore it.

He frowned, his bewilderment fading.

The veiled warrior didn't react to any of them. Rather, he kept his weapon locked against Aaron's.

"The chief's boy," he said at last. His voice was cold, but there was the softest hint of a smile somewhere within it. Rivulets of water ran down the snout of his mask to roll over his menacing grin. "Not the royal I was expecting to see."

With a heavy shove, Aaron forced him back. He didn't get the chance to question him, for another voice sounded above the rain:

"Renée!"

At the call Renée looked up and saw Mekial running to her with Dillon, Klarys and Lacey right behind him. Kurt was on Dillon's back and like Lilian, all of them were covered in filth. Other than that, they were unharmed.

"Mekial!" Renée ran to meet him and hugged him.

Crying out, the rest of the children ran to their group.

Recognizing that this was some kind of reunion, the masked warrior cut his sword through the rainy air and sheathed it.

Aaron lowered his tonfa, but he didn't put them away.*tv*

"I'm glad you guys're okay," Brent said, kneeling before Dillon, Klarys and Lacey.

The girls paused. Then they threw their arms around him and started to cry.

Dillon silently leaned into the group hug as well.

"What happened to Kurt?" Aaron asked.

Dillon straightened up with a grim look. "He passed out earlier. We think he inhaled too much smoke. We've gotta get him to Khirsta…"

"What happened to you?" Putting away her sword, Renée tried scrubbing Mekial's face clean with the rain. "Why did you leave Taranis? You know it's dangerous in the Empire! You're just a trainee! What were you thinking?!"

"I know, I was stupid," Mekial admitted, crestfallen. "But, we got lucky…that guy saved us."

Renée turned to see the man who'd attacked Aaron once more. Mekial felt her tense beside him. "Who is he?"

"I don't know. He didn't say his name." Mekial dropped his voice to a whisper. "But he knows about Taranis. And the raiders."

Brent, Aaron and Liam, having overheard this aside, looked at the swordsman sharply.

Kurt groaned.

Brent and everyone else turned to see him stir atop Dillon's shoulders. A moment later, he blinked his eyes open wearily and coughed.

"Are we out yet…?" His voice was a terrible croak.

His friends shared soft smiles of relief.

"Yeah," Dillon told him. "We made it out of the fire."

Kurt's eyes wandered across the glum landscape and revolved to the blue-haired Avat in front of him. "Brent…?" He sent him a lopsided smile and strained to look around more. "Aaron…and Liam, too…" His eyelids began to droop. "See, Dill, I…I told you they'd…see the signal…" He slipped away, unconscious once more.

Dillon started. "Kurt? Kurt, wake up! Kurt!"

Brent plucked the child off of his back and placed him on his own. "Aaron, how long will it take for me to get to the Skycrafts from here would you say?"

"Not long, if you sprint the whole way," Aaron answered. "Go through those trees." He tipped his head.

"Got it. I'm flying ahead to bring him to Khirsta. I'll see you guys back home." Without sparing another second, he hurried off.

"Flying?" Dillon mumbled and he exchanged quizzical looks with Klarys and Lacey.

"Thank you," Renée said abruptly, her eyes on the masked warrior. "For helping them."

"Just consider it a passing favor," the swordsman said.

Aaron cut to a different point. "Are you the 'extra' that we heard about?"

"Extra?" The warrior paused. His voice was stiff when he next spoke. "I suppose."

"Because you're more than that, aren't you?" Aaron didn't feel like ignoring what was obvious. "You're Saruke's Shade."

Without a word, the man bowed theatrically. Lifting his head, he cocked it to the side to show that he suspected that Aaron had more to say.

"Saruke's Shade?" Renée repeated, painfully aware of her own ignorance.

"What're you doing all the way in Lyrik?" Aaron continued, ignoring her.

"Me? I just like to cause a stir." The man straightened up. "I don't like imperials. But I do enjoy making their lives as miserable as they've made mine."

"So there's no real point to anything you've done besides your own satisfaction."

The man held up a gloved finger. "Nailed it in one."

Aaron tightened his grip on his tonfa.

Liam noticed. "We owe him," he said, coming level with him.

Aaron viewed him out of the side of his eye. When he looked to Saruke's Shade again, his gaze lingered on the insignia on the mask's forehead.

"Maybe you should take the other Skycraft and fly the kids back," Liam went on, sensing Aaron's rebellion.

Aaron looked from him to Lilian. "...You do it. I don't think Lil likes the idea of being separated from you again."

Though Lilian didn't respond, the way she inched closer to Liam spoke for her.

"You can still catch Brent if you go now," he said. "He can take the ones who don't fit with you."

"Go with them, Mekial," Renée said to him. "I'll see you at home."

"Okay...wait! I almost forgot to tell you!" Mekial's face lit up. "I figured out the truth, Ren! I'm an aetheriest! Actually, I'm innate!"

When Khirsta finished spreading her oil and herb mixture across Kurt's small chest, she leaned back to look him over.

He was sleeping in one of the beds in her hut, his crazy curls pushed away from his brow and his body limp with fatigue. His breathing was no longer ragged and soft but had evened out well since she'd begun to apply the medicine, and his face had been washed clean. The redness in his cheeks had faded and though his eyebrows were still partly furrowed, he didn't appear to be in nearly as much distress as he'd been in before.

Khirsta set the bowl that held her strong-scented concoction on the stand beside her, satisfied with her work. "As his friends thought, he did inhale a lot of smoke," she confirmed. "It's likely what made his lungs constrict and caused him to pass out. But the medicine should clear his airways nicely. I expect that he'll be stable by tomorrow." She turned to see Brent, who was leaning against the wall opposite the boy's bed with his arms folded. "I'll watch over him until then. But I'd like to see the other children as well. I know you sent them home to give Kurt some space, but I should make sure they're all okay."

Brent's eyes were on the earthen floor. It was impossible to tell if he was even listening.

"What about you?" she asked, squinting at him.

He looked up. "Me? I'm fine."

"No…" Khirsta rose from her chair and approached him. She studied his tired, muddy face with the concern of an aged mother. "Something is wrong."

Brent avoided her stare.

Something *was* wrong. Even after he'd left his friends and the masked swordsman behind, he was plagued with a peculiar sense of familiarity with the stranger. Or at least, his appearance.

He couldn't reason out why it bothered him so much, though. He'd tried to dismiss it from his mind when Liam had met him with the rest of the children, and had managed to ignore it long enough to figure out an arrangement so they could fly the little ones back to Taranis safely.

But as soon as they'd gone airborne it came back to him and still now, it lingered.

But he didn't want to bother Khirsta with it.

He pushed off the wall. "It's nothing. I'll be back to check on him later. And I'll let the others know they need to come see you." His eyes averted, he left, leaving Khirsta to look on after him in troubled concern.

Outside, Brent descended to a lower part of the moonlit road and soon noticed how empty the village looked. He'd been in such a hurry to bring Kurt to Khirsta that he hadn't noticed at all.

It seemed that everyone was still sheltering inside.

His golden eyes wandered down the hill, and soon landed on Greta's hut. He approached it, and was just feet away from the door when Liam came out.

He wasn't at all surprised to see Brent standing across from him.

"How is she?" Brent asked.

Liam's near-white eyes moved away. "…She's not hurt," he said after a moment. His hand lingered on the doorknob. "But, she's still upset."

Brent nodded absently, not sure what to say.

Liam faced him. "How's Kurt?"

"Still unconscious. But Khirsta said she'll be fine."

"Right." Liam paused, thinking. "…Brent."

"Yeah?"

"That man in the mask. You know him?"

"No." Brent shook his head. "At least…I don't think so."

Liam's face, though still difficult for Brent to decipher no matter how long they'd known each other, offered him a hint of suspicion.

He rubbed the back of his head. "I just…I get the feeling that I might know him from somewhere but, I can't put my finger on it."

Liam didn't respond.

Brent cast his eyes to the fields beyond the farmlands. A hint of movement had caught his attention.

The aetheriests were making their way back to Taranis aboard their saigas, he soon realized, for he could spot the yellow-haired creatures in the shadowy recesses of the valley near the barrier that separated it from Odelwhite.

While he couldn't see the details of the group's faces, Brent figured that Aaron and Renée were among the party. It was likely that the masked swordsman was with them as well.

"Looks like they're coming back," he said.

Liam made a short humming sound to offer his acknowledgement.

"How're Kurt and the others?" Aaron asked when he and the other villagers reached Taranis, and he slid off the saiga that he'd been sharing with Kyrah.

"Fine," Brent responded. "Khirsta's taking care of Kurt, and the rest went home. She wants all of them to check in with her though, just in case."

"Dad's probably gonna want us to come in to get debriefed along with the aetheriests and scouts," Aaron figured as he came nearer. "He and Mom had the other raiders stay behind to guard the village. He'll wanna know why we weren't around."

Brent tipped his chin in understanding.

"I want to check on Mekial," Renée said, slipping down from behind Aizen. She walked towards them. "Do you think you'll be able to stand in for me?"

Aaron, Brent and Liam looked at one another.

"Fine," Aaron said with a raising of his shoulder. "I doubt he'll need all of us, anyway."

Alerted to movement elsewhere, Brent flicked his eyes upward in time to see the nameless swordsman get down from the saiga he'd been sitting on.

Without a word the man walked past him and examined the wooden community for a space of silence. With the glowing light of the moon and its empty roads, it was almost eerie to look at.

"…It really has grown," he said finally.

He sounded distant. Seeing the village seemed to have transported his mind elsewhere.

"Do you really have to keep that mask on?" Kyrah asked, moving towards him. "We're outside of the Empire now. No one here will think to endanger you if they know who you are."

"I know." The warrior reached for his mask and removed it, revealing a pair of piercing, cobalt eyes and a head of thick, black hair that was nearly flattened against his scalp. A short beard was growing across his chiseled cheeks and with a nostalgic smile, he scratched it. "It's just been a while…" Lowering the fiendish mask to his hip, where its mane dangled past his knees, he turned to face the group.

Brent's thoughts screeched to a halt.

Lemm smirked, amused by his wide-eyed stare. "Hasn't it, kid?"

67

EMM SQUATTED IN *front of the kitchen cupboard, his face flat.*

His eleven-year-old body tucked in the depths of the cabinet, Brent tried to wedge himself deeper into it.

Lemm's face was still deadpan. "What're you doing?"

Brent whimpered pathetically.

Lemm sighed softly and rubbed his eyes before looking at him again. "What's your name, kid?"

"B…Brent…"

"Brent?"

Brent nodded hurriedly.

"Okay. I'm Lemm." The young man, barely past his late teens, lifted his chin. "So, listen, my neighbor just showed up, looking for you I'm guessing, so I'll just tell him you're here, you can go back with him, and we can both get back to our lives."

He stood and Brent gaped after him. Just before Lemm could exit the room, he flew out of the cupboard and snatched the hem of his tunic. "No, don't!"

Lemm turned with a heated scowl.

"Adelle told me to find you," the boy blurted. "She said you could help me. So please, don't tell Mr. Scott!" His eyes watered. "Don't tell him!"

His sight blurring, he started to scrub his face and cleanse them of tears. But no matter how many he wiped away, more took their place.

"…My cousin sent you to me." Lemm let those words sink in. Looking Brent over, he did a double-take to his pointy ears.

He shook his head, and his jaw clenched with immediate anger. "She always does this to me…sending Avats my way like I'm some kind of…" A stream of curses left his mouth and he ended it all with a huff. "You're goin' back."

"I-I can't." Brent stepped away from him, anxious and still teary-eyed.

"Why not?"

"Because she got caught by slave traders…" His face crumpled again. "And it's my fault…"

"Caught by —?" Lemm raised his eyebrows and then shook his head vexedly. "Oh, great. Of course. I should've seen this coming. I should've known she was gonna get herself caught!"

"I'm sorry…" Brent sniffed.

Lemm leaned against the kitchen counter, fuming and silent.

"Please…" Brent begged and Lemm peered at him over his shoulder. His empty look from earlier had returned. "She said to come to you…"

"…Fine, kid." Lemm straightened up and turned on him fully. "You can count yourself lucky."

Brent started to smile, relieved.

Lemm dropped a bombshell: "We're getting my cousin."

Brent's mouth fell open all over again. "W-we are…?!"

"Yep. Cuz I ain't helpin' you."

Brent blinked in obvious confusion.

Ignoring him, Lemm crossed into the next room over and opened up a side door. When he entered, Brent peeked in after him.

There wasn't much there. But atop a crate in the corner, he did spy something of interest: a wooden mask with a lion-like snout, a dagger-toothed grin, black eyes, a wild mane of hair…and there, on its forehead, was a strange symbol. One of interlocking rings and disconnected lines.

He frowned.

Blocking Brent's face with his hand, Lemm pushed him out of the room —

And Brent's eyes reopened in the present.

Arms folded, he was leaning against one of the walls of the conference room. Ivan, Xëri, Heldar, Aaron, Liam and Aizen were also present.

All of them had their eyes on Lemm.

It had been seven years since Brent had last seen him. He certainly hadn't been expecting to cross paths with him ever again, and definitely not under the current circumstances.

He glanced at Lemm's mask, which was now hooked to his left shoulder. The mane looped around his neck like the mantle of a cloak.

It was definitely the same one that he'd noticed in Lemm's side room all those years ago. He wondered how long the man had had it. More so than that, he wondered where it came from for, now that he considered it, it reminded him of the masked stranger that he and Liam had encountered outside of Cleopa.

Moreover, on their way to the Arkanian Prune Plateau with Eklaire, Aaron had shared with him the rumors of a masked character that was wreaking havoc across the Empire. According to him, Arkania currently knew this criminal as "Saruke's Shade", and Chief Ivan had shared that his grinning mask had been modeled after alleged descriptions of the mysterious Çaru'qu. Given the uncanny similarity between their names, Aaron had considered it as good a lead as they were going to get when it came to determining the meaning behind that masked stranger's words in Lenora.

So, Brent thought it rather convenient that that lead would suddenly show up at their doorstep.

His eyes tightened with suspicion.

"...Your scouts learned about the guardsmen's attack a few weeks ago," Lemm was saying, and he caught sight of Brent's quiet glare. He only acknowledged it with a smirk — one that could have just as easily been an accent to his present monogue. Indeed, the interaction had been so short that it was hardly noticed by anyone. "Then they scrambled to find help, and eventually ran into me. As soon as we knew the details of the operation, we tailed the imperials and offered our services of...extracting them from the area.

"But as close as we were to this cozy little village," he turned to face everyone with a strange smile, "I wasn't expecting to actually stop by. But, who doesn't like surprises?"

He received nothing more than a line-up of empty expressions.

He scoffed, humored. "What?"

Brent looked away.

"All right…" Lemm teased his hair into a messy pompadour. "What's the problem? Something in my teeth?"

Ivan shifted a little and his eyes slid to Brent.

Brent caught his wandering gaze for a fleeting second. He looked away just as quickly.

"Is just that…we have not seen you in seven years," Ivan said deliberately and his gaze returned to Lemm at a disbelieving squint, as if he'd suddenly realized how long it'd been. "And now, sudden-ly…you are here, arriving at debrief with scouts that many believed were gone. And…" He paused delicately. "I…heard what happened to your property. Even I believed that you were lost to us."

Brent's eyebrows twitched with confusion, but he didn't speak.

Lemm's smile became absent, like he was waiting to see if there was something else Ivan wanted to add. When he saw that there wasn't, he tipped his head nonchalantly. "Well, you're welcome. For saving Taranis. And apparently," he added good-naturedly, "for bringing back the dead."

Ivan's frown deepened. "Heldar," he said gruffly, and he granted the head aetheriest his attention. "Report."

"Sir," Heldar acknowledged. "The destruction in Odelwhite Forest is mostly restricted to the Revere Falls region. Luckily, it didn't spread to the barrier that blocks the way into the valley. But if the fires had lasted a little longer, it'd be a different story. We're lucky the rains came when they did. So far as I know, that's what put out the fires. As far as the guardsmen go, all were defeated, and their aetheriests likely died from overexposure to the aether. Many of their bodies were found to have suffered a quintessent overload."

Brent, Aaron and Liam shared quick looks, but said nothing.

Aizen was hard-faced, eyes forward.

"Still, that doesn't mean we're not without severe damages elsewhere," Heldar continued. "A lot of the underground tunnels that we use to escort roaming runaways into Taranis are in danger of collapsing, if they haven't already. Given the village's precarious situation, rebuilding them might have to wait."

Ivan made a low grumbling sound in the back of his throat. "How many guardsmen were there?"

"At least sixty, give or take."

Xëri's forehead crinkled.

"And you are sure they are all gone?" Ivan asked.

"Yes, sir. I've left a few of our aetheriests out there to clear out the bodies. They should be done long before anyone arrives to investigate the region."

Ivan scowled at nothing for a minute, considering. "This attack," he said at last, "is why you did not reach out to Taranis for past month." He looked at Aizen.

"Yes, sir." Aizen's low voice vibrated through the walls. "We didn't know how they managed to get an idea of Taranis' location, so we ceased communications in case it would further jeopardize the village's safety. We apologize for any grief it may've caused."

"Grief?" Ivan echoed gravely, his bright eyes trained on him. "Yes…this caused us much grief, Aizen."

Aizen stood straight and tall, but not even his manner of being could detract from the guilt that Ivan's words had inflicted on him.

"But, I understand you were acting in Taranis' best interest," the chief continued, "out of concern for everyone here."

His eyes skipped over to Lemm, who was watching Aizen with a glimmer of amusement.

Distrust tugged at the skin around Ivan's eyes.

"So," Aaron picked up, "you guys scoured Taranis' area of operations in Lyrik to find someone who could help you deal with the imperials, and you found this guy." He nodded at Lemm. "What's your name again?"

"Lemm," the newcomer told him. "And I used to work with the big ol' Brusseirian Bear over there." He tipped his head in Ivan's direction. "I'm one of the veteran raiders, you could say. And as for him," Lemm looked at Brent, "we go way back. Don't we?"

Brent turned his eyes from Lemm without a sound.

"Aw, don't be like that." Lemm's voice rose with mockery. "And here I thought we were friends."

While he'd been trying to keep silent for the duration of the debriefing session, Brent couldn't hold back at that. "Yeah. I thought the same, until you blamed me for Adelle's death and cut ties with us altogether."

A sharp silence followed. Even Lemm found himself speechless for a moment.

He finally broke the tension with a dry laugh and shook his head, his eyes lowering for a second. They flipped up darkly. "You expectin' an apology?"

"No." Brent unfolded his arms. "That's in the past."

Lemm raised an eyebrow with a dry smile.

"But I do expect you to tell us why you bothered to help save the village at all. From what I remember, you didn't want anything to do with us before."

Lemm shrugged, the corners of his lips curving down carelessly. "A guy can't have a change of heart?"

Brent's eyes tightened and his jaw clenched, daring Lemm to provoke him further.

"Oh, you want the full story?" Lemm raised an eyebrow. "All right. I'll give you the full story." He inclined his head to Aizen. "I met your friend here and one other scout near my hometown not even two or three weeks back. They'd already been following leads on the invasion by that point. We dug a little deeper, spoke to some other supporters, and it turned out the Empire's been tracking your movements for years. All their intel was connected to reports of 'strange activity' near the southwestern borders of Lyrik. Over time one report led to another, and the next thing they knew they were on track to figuring out that some of the savages they wanted so badly were probably living near Odelwhite.

"I'd imagine that your aethericsts have managed to hold them and even regular soldiers off until now, what with their creating illusions to scare imperials away when they get too close to Taranis' secret entrance. Right?" Lemm looked at Ivan and Xëri for confirmation, but he didn't wait for it. "Rumors about Odelwhite being haunted are all over the place these days. But, I guess the consistency of the slave traders' reports finally pushed Empyrean's Guard to do what needed to be done. And as it turns out, torching the forest is a lot more efficient than wading through it for clues." He smiled darkly.

"They definitely went all out," Heldar ruminated, his eyes lowering pensively. "But, there's still something that's bothering me."

"You mean besides the fact that Taranis was almost burnt to the ground?" Aaron asked.

"The aetheriests that they had," Heldar said, ignoring Aaron's remark. "They were using element armigers. Krogan claimed to have witnessed as much, and said so when I and the other aetheriests arrived. But, I didn't believe him until I actually saw it."

Xëri blinked, startled. "Are you sure that's what they were using?"

Heldar nodded. "There's no doubt about it."

Xëri's troubled frown spoke for her. Her eyes fell to the table.

"I'm sure you all know the one," Heldar continued and he looked at everyone else. "An element armiger is what allows an aetheriest to completely encase his body in whatever element that he wants, to put it simply. Records claim that the only ones capable of pulling off stunts like that were the aetherians, but no one's seen any of them since the Third Aether War. Which begs the question as to how Empyrean's Guard was able to pull off this sort of attack to begin with. I myself am suspicious that they've been secretly building up an army of aetherians."

"What about witches and warlocks?" Liam countered evenly. "In the Empire, witches can brew potions that can artificially enhance someone's quintessence. Warlocks can do the same thing by inhaling ground up stones from the Lenoran mines. Think the guardsmen used something like that?"

"That's certainly possible. It was brought to my attention that Empyrean's Guard has managed to get their hands on some sort of elixir that works similar to that." As he scanned the room, Heldar's eyes jumped from Aaron to the chief. "There have also been rumors that the Empire has been conducting experiments in the hopes of creating a more powerful version of the witch's drink. I suppose what we saw in Odelwhite could be considered evidence of those rumors. But we were lucky — although they were definitely executing element armigers, the guardsmen's skill level wasn't that of an aetherian. Their strength was artificial, which was their own undoing."

"Luck. Again," Aaron grunted.

Brent thought of the blue-haired man that had saved them at the last second.

Luck indeed.

"As for you three." Ivan looked between Brent, Aaron and Liam. "Harver came to me to explain where you had gone, and why, and how. Are the children safe?"

"Yes," Aaron answered.

"Liam and I brought them back," Brent said. "Kurt was in the worst shape, but Khirsta's taking care of him. She said he'll be stable by tomorrow."

"Good. What of Renée?"

"She's all right. She wanted to check on Mekial."

"Hm. And scouts and aetheriests?" Ivan's eyes revolved to everyone else. "Do we have any casualties?"

"Half of our aetheriests are wounded," Heldar replied, "including the brothers, and Kyrah. But, they should recover after a few days."

"With the exception of three, all scouts are accounted for," Aizen assured him. "Two more are critically injured."

Ivan dipped his bearded face gravely. "Understood. Then, the rest of you must prioritize rest. We do not know when or if Empire will strike us again. We need everyone in best shape. Lemm," Ivan faced him. "What will you do now?"

"Yeah, layin' low's probably a good idea." Lemm stroked his stubbly chin. "If you wouldn't mind lendin' me a room in one of those fancy new apartment buildings you've got, well, I'd certainly be willin' take you up on it."

Ivan nodded and his eyes jumped to Aaron. "Show Lemm to space where he can stay in the new apartments."

Aaron cast Lemm a short look. "Understood."

"Xëri," Ivan looked at her next, "send word throughout village that the people may leave their homes. But, they must not leave Taranis under any circumstances."

"All right," she agreed.

"Meanwhile, I will convene with the head council," Ivan finished. "We will discuss next course of action for Taranis, and I will gather everyone at later time to issue new orders." He dipped his bearded chin roughly. "Dismissed."

Aaron didn't wait around. With a silent nod in Lemm's direction, he vacated the conference room with the long-lost supporter going after him.

Brent didn't look at him when he went by.

Outside the night air was cool, and Aaron could catch slices of conversation issuing from peoples' huts and houses, for the villagers were still restless after the evening's events. Here and there, children stuck their heads out of windows to see him before being ushered away by their parents. Elsewhere villagers pulled their windows shut, allowing only a sliver of candlelight to break through the shutters.

"This whole place has changed," Lemm said, breaking the quiet that had settled between them, and he tossed his shining blue eyes to the cozy little cabins, then to the stream, then to the farmlands that rested below. He smirked. "Never thought I'd see it get this big in my day."

Aaron didn't respond.

"Wonder what happened?" Lemm called, clearly meaning to pull the raider into conversation. "Changed tactics, I'm guessing."

"Something like that." Aaron kept walking and he turned down a side path that led to the apartments. "Guess you could say it all started when Brent joined the frontlines."

"Heh. So after all that, the kid became the hometown hero." Lemm looked around again. "Who'da thunk."

Aaron was silent.

In just a few short minutes, they reached the yard that expanded in front of the U-shaped apartments. Several of its windows were dark; the tenants were either asleep or were keeping their lights low until everything was confirmed to be safe.

Here, Aaron stopped walking. "…Now I've got a question."

Stopping behind him, Lemm awaited his inquiry.

"Earlier, when you saw me." Aaron circled to face him. "You said I wasn't the 'royal' you were expecting to see. What were you talking about?"

"I said that?" Lemm rubbed his chin and looked up with an almost crafty eye. "Hm. Curious."

Aaron's eyebrow twitched. His glower remained.

Lemm noticed, and he dropped his hand with a quiet sound of laughter. "Y'know, I used to work real close with a lot of people here." A twinkle entered his eye. "One thing I learned pretty quick: even the ones closest to you have got secrets. Secrets that you could never come up with yourself."

Aaron's frown was steadfast.

"Sometimes, kid," Lemm started forward, "you have to step away from it all, to find out what the truth really is. Even the truth of what you might really be." He came level with Aaron, shoulder-to-shoulder. The redhead himself only followed him out of the corner of his eye. "You can only live in a utopia like this for so long before even you start to notice that something might be missing."

"What," Aaron's frown deepened, "are you trying to say?"

Lemm smiled crookedly, and he looked on at the doors of the apartment. Sarcasm was heavy in his next statement. "Seeing you now, it almost brings me to tears. The youth are raised on nothing but lies, and the ones in charge don't even think to correct it.

"Even your old pal Skylok is living a lie." He looked at him. "'The Avat Prince', as some people have been calling him."

Aaron snorted. "What, you're trying to say that *Brent's* the royal you were looking for? Please — if he's an imperial prince, my uncle's a flying rabbit-monkey."

Lemm chuckled gently and walked away. "Like I said: even the ones closest to you have got secrets.

"Even your scouting buddies have told me that you've got a habit of sneaking out into the Empire all on your own. All to find answers to things that you know you can't find in here." Stopping, he turned his head, but he didn't completely look at Aaron over his shoulder.

In answer to his statement, Aaron had pressed his lips together. He didn't say anything.

"But as long as you choose to keep coming back to this place, held under your father's thumb…and even your mother's…"

Turning away, Lemm peered into the sky.

"I wonder how much longer all of you will last." He sounded strange now, distant.

Aaron shifted, turning to face him, and as he did Lemm spoke again.

"Still, maybe there's hope for you yet. After all," the swordsman finally looked at him, a certain gleam in his eye and a shadow of laughter in his dark smile, "even the biggest lies…are grounded in truth."

Aaron's scowl returned, but this time it was touched with doubt. Even, a hint of unease.

"Heh." Lemm walked away. He lifted a hand in farewell. "The guest rooms are on the ground floor, aren't they? We can part ways here."

Thus did he leave Aaron by himself, with the wind creeping past his toes and rolling through his hair.*tv*

❧ ✢ ❧

When her bucket was full, Renée hefted it out of the stream with a gentle grunt. Her trained muscles tensed and with it in hand, she circled to return home.

Her ponytail swung delicately as she went, and she caught something shift in the side of her vision. She checked to see what it was.

Kro was standing not too far from her. He hadn't yet changed, and he still looked just as exhausted as he had earlier. He swayed dangerously.

"Kro!" Putting her bucket down, she went and steadied him. "What're you doing on your feet? You should be back in your room, resting!"

Kro winced. Planting a hand on her shoulder, he righted himself. "I'll be fine," he sighed. "I just…came to tell you something."

Her round eyes glinted curiously. She waited.

"I…uh…" His cheeks turned beet-red. Flustered, guilt-ridden and annoyed with himself, he couldn't look her in the face any

THE AVAT PRINCE
CODE: IMPERIAL

longer. "I'm sorry!"

Her eyebrows wrinkled in confusion. "Why?"

Kro raked a hand through his hair. "Mekial…and all of his friends," he started. "They were in the Empire…because of me."

Renée's frown slowly morphed into alarmed caution. "What do you mean?"

He took a breath. "I told Mekial…that the only way to find out if he was really an aetheriest was if he met me at Revere Falls. He brought his friends with him. So we were all out there together when the guardsmen showed up."

No words left Renée's mouth, for her voice was stifled by her own stupefaction. At long last, her soundless expression tightened into a fiery glare.

Kro gulped.

⤞ ⚜ ⤝

As soon as he stepped over the threshold of his home, Aaron suddenly noticed how tired he felt. He could've dropped to the floor and slept soundly.

Crossing into the rearmost room of the house, he bathed using the wash bins that were there. When he came back out, he wasn't at all surprised to see his mother in the connecting corridor. He'd heard her come in after all.

"Hey, Mom."

"Aaron!" She looked up from her dreary thoughts tiredly. "I thought you'd still be out."

"Doesn't take that long to drop someone off at the apartments." Aaron tightened his pants about his toned waist and dried his damp hair with the patterned cloth that he'd laid on his head. "Is Dad still meeting with the head council?"

"Yes…" Xëri's weary look returned. "The way it's going, he might be there for the rest of the night."

"Oh."

"I'm glad you're safe," she added. "Eklaire had told me that you'd gone to the fires. I was angry at first, but, when she said why…" She smiled tenderly and came near to him. Bringing his head to her level, she brushed his bangs aside to kiss his brow. "I'm proud of you. And I'm so glad that you all brought Mekial and his friends back safely."

"Yeah…" Aaron went back to drying his head. The cloth he was using cast a small shadow over his distant, blue-eyed face. "Hey, that guy, Lemm…Dad told me that Adelle was his cousin?"

"…Yes." Xëri's voice was remote, as if her mind had drifted into days long passed. "He was one of the first Arkanians to offer us his help, along with Adelle. He comes off as rude and detached but, his heart is as good as hers."

Aaron didn't make a sound, not entirely interested in the latter half of his mother's description. "We ran into him in the woods. He had Mekial and the others with him." A forbidding shadow passed over his face. "And…he called me a royal."

Xëri stiffened and her eyes darted away. "Did he? That's odd."

Aaron noticed her strange reaction. "…Maybe it's cuz I'm the chief's son."

Xëri actually laughed, her discomfort leaving her. "I don't think that quite equates you to the status of a nobleman, Aaron."

"Maybe it could." His lazy smile soon fell away to be replaced with a slow and pensive frown. "He said something else after that: that he hadn't been expecting to run into a royal like me. It almost sounded like he'd been expecting to bump into a different one." He looked her in the eye. "I think he believes all those rumors that went around earlier, about Brent being related to the imperial royal family."

Xëri frowned a little, inquisitive but also perplexed.

Aaron's eyes narrowed thoughtfully. "Did you believe them?"

"Hm? Of course not." Xëri offered up a pale, unbelievable smile. "Brent, a prince?"

"Yeah…crazy." Aaron looked away. "Still…heard it got so serious that even the viceroy had to make a statement."

"Now there's something. Although…" Xeri twisted her lip. "It is strange…Brent is the only Avat I've ever met who has blue hair and golden eyes. The only other people in the world who look like that are…"

Aaron frowned, bothered.

Xëri was quiet.

At last, Aaron released an irritated grunt. "Ugh, forget it, I'm way too tired for this!"

Xëri smiled with a hopeless shake of her head. "Get some rest, Aaron. You've earned it."

"Yeah…" Bidding her good night, he dragged himself into his room and shut the door.

Xëri went upstairs to her own bed, where she curled up atop it and settled in to sleep.

But her eyes wouldn't close.

On the level below her, Aaron stared at the ceiling as he lay in his bed.

His eyes wouldn't close, either.

❦

"Well? Feel like you did your good deed for the day?" Viorë'to skipped behind Oruviçu, who was standing in the shadow of a pine on the edge of the valley. His supernatural eyes were fixed on Taranis. "Wonder how the Elder'll feel about it."

"I'm sure he'll approve," Oruviçu said, "since it meant the sparing of his grandson. And as for the other…I understand why you hate him." He finally tilted to see his ally. "But in the face of what may come, biases will be of no use to us."

Viorë'to scoffed. When she replied, her voice was colder than a winter frost. "Y'know…you're a real a hypocrite."

Oruviçu didn't answer. He only looked out to Taranis again.

Behind him, Viorë'to vanished into the darkness as if she'd never even been there at all.

68

L EMM HADN'T BEEN expecting the amari tree hill to be as quiet as it was when he got there, in the dead of night. He was used to there being a sound whenever he showed up: the twitter of birds, the whisper of wind — the twinkling laugh of his dear cousin.

But now, not even the crickets were singing.

In this transcendent quiet, he crossed the grassy hill that surrounded the tree. The air was still, though not hot, and rays of silver light glistened through the leafy, pink vines. The moon itself denoted the hour of midnight.

He sighed when he reached the trailing branches, and looked upon the rock that would forever mark Adelle's resting place. Dropping to one knee, he balanced his arm across his thigh.

With his eyebrows arching, the sides of his lips curled into a genuine, but sad smile. "Some cousin I am. Hope you don't mind a visit that's seven years overdo."

A small breeze went by, lifting the tree's drooping vines. Several petals broke free to drift into the night.

Lemm's gentle smile remained. "I wish I could stay and tell you everything, Adelle. Everything that's happened between then and now." His lips twitched humorously. "I wonder what you'd say if you could hear it. Scold me one more time, I bet."

He paused. Then, reaching out, he touched the headstone. "I'm gonna make everything right. I want you to know that much at least." He blinked away his rising emotion. "Just you wait. Okay?"

Footsteps crunched across the ground behind him.

His face falling, Lemm peered over his shoulder.

Ivan had appeared at the edge of the wood.

Standing, Lemm faced him. "I thought you had some meeting to get to."

"We have finished." Ivan didn't react to Lemm's clear annoyance for his arrival. "Is well past midnight. Entire village is asleep. After what happened today, I thought you would be doing the same."

Lemm smiled with a crafty gleam in his moonlit eyes. "Likewise. At least I got in a power-nap."

Ivan lowered his gaze to the fiendish mask that was still hooked to the man's shoulder. "…I am surprised you still have that," he said.

Lemm laughed and he patted the fearsome accessory. "Well, why not? It was a gift. Consider me a sentimentalist."

Ivan's bushy brows knit together and he tilted his head to view him askance. "Why are you really here, Lemmiere?"

Lemm's face dropped, a nerve clearly having been touched by the utterance of his full name. Finally, he sighed. "Y'know, it kinda hurts that even you don't trust me, Chief. I came to help some old friends. Taranis is like a second home to me. I'm not so horrible that I'd let it go up in smoke."

Ivan grunted quietly.

Lemm heard it and when he looked at him again, the glimmer in his eye had taken on a glow of tickled interest. It was like he was playing a game and had finally found someone that could match his cunning. "What? You don't believe me?"

Ivan examined him scrupulously. "You…have changed, Lemm," he said at last. "There is something different about you. Is…disturbing."

"Heh." Lemm thrust his chin out. "Time does that to people. You look like you've packed on a few pounds, yourself. Lady Xëri's been takin' good care of you, I see."

Ivan's eyes narrowed.

"What? You can laugh." Lemm tilted his head and rubbed his chin, his teeth gleaming in a crooked smile. "It's funny."

Ivan decided to continue. "I have not forgotten how you left us," he said. "I have come to ask that you do not give Brent any trouble."

Lemm dropped his hand back to his side. His unhinged amusement was still apparent. "Why would I give him any trouble? I've managed to get my closure." His smile widened. "Unless there's somethin' about him that I should know?"

Ivan didn't move, but a flicker in his eyes suggested a muted idea that he wasn't willing to share.

"Or maybe you just care a lot about him. I heard from your scouts that you took him in, since he didn't have anyone to live in the apartments with." Lemm's eyes twinkled. "Or do I really seem like the kind of guy who'd cause grief for some kid?"

"Lemm…" Ivan allowed concern to peek through his stern visage. "What happened to you? After the imperials came to your home."

Lemm scoffed, his face falling. But the ice in his cobalt gaze had hardened.

"I was informed…that your property was burned to the ground, three years ago."

"What do you think happened, Chief? I got sold into slavery, like the big, bad co-conspirator that I am." Lemm's dangerous smile returned. "Then, I broke out. Salvaged some good ol' keepsakes from back home, and took off to Nassaul for a bit. Ain't been to this side of the Empire in…what, a year since then? Pretty nostalgic."

"Saruke's Shade."

Lemm cocked an eyebrow.

"This is name the Empire has been calling you, yes?" Ivan made a small gesture with his hand. "Aaron is very thorough scout to have learned this. News of you has not reached the public here yet."

Lemm pointed at him and something glittered in his eyes. Whether it was intrigue or an urge to do harm was difficult to tell. "I am quite proud of that. Sure, those dumb imperials botched the name, but" — he shrugged — "it's the thought that counts. And it sounds like you and Xëri raised a smart kid," he continued. "And you scored another bonus with the other one. What do they call him now?" He tapped his chin. "Oh, yeah: Skylok, right?"

Ivan didn't respond for a moment.

"I…have said my piece," he said at last and he stepped away to show that he meant to leave. "You are welcome to stay in Taranis for as long as you need. But, if you should cause any trouble, I will have to make you leave."

Turning away, the chief strode between the trees to return to the village.

Lemm watched him go without a word. All that betrayed his emotions were the gleam in his eye and the slight rise of the corner of his mouth.

⁓ ✢ ⁓

"Uncle…?"

Lilian's tiny voice, pitched to a soft whine, pulled Liam from his dreamless sleep.

Rolling over, he picked up the lantern that was by his sleeping mat and sat up. After he'd switched it on, he got to his feet and shuffled to the other side of the straw divider that walled off his sleeping space.

"What is it, Lil?" he asked foggily, sitting by her.

She was half-hidden beneath her pillows and stuffed animals. The qalimba wasn't far from them. "I'm scared…I had a night-mare…"

"It's okay, Lil…it was just a dream…" His silver eyes finally adjusted to the poor lighting and he squinted to see her face.

It looked like she'd been crying.

Immediately, he understood. "Was it about the fire?"

She nodded and sniffed. "Can you tell me a story? Something about Mommy." Though her eyelids were drooping, she refused to fall back asleep. "Every time I close my eyes, I keep seeing fire and bodies…all those dead bodies…"

Liam's brow crinkled and he touched her face. "You're safe now, Lil. There's no fire anymore. And the imperials are all gone."

"I know…Mekial saved us, but…"

"Mekial?"

She bobbed her head again. "We were with Kro, and then the guardsmen came…he protected us, but then more guardsmen showed up. But then, Mekial beat them both and he saved us again. I think he made a cold wind once, too, because one time we were surrounded by fire. But then a cold wind came out of nowhere and blew it all away."

Liam stared at her, his irises shaking as he went over her story. He blinked, frowning. "How'd he do any of that?"

"Kro said it's because he's an aetheriest. The guy in the mask said the same thing."

Liam raised his eyebrows. He'd heard Mekial reveal that to Renée, but he hadn't believed it.

"Wait, why were you out there with Kro?" he blurted, feeling like he was missing a key point to the story.

"I don't wanna talk about it anymore," Lilian said, her voice tired with exhaustion. "It's your turn to tell a story."

"Lilian."

The little girl stared at him, her lips shifting soundlessly. At last, she surrendered the details. "Mekial wanted to find out if he was an aetheriest, because he kept being able to do weird things, like with the entelodon, and moving stuff without touching them. So me and the others went with him to meet Kro at Revere Falls, so Kro could train him."

"So you were out there because of Kro."

Lilian nodded quietly.

Liam turned away, his face unreadable.

"Uncle…" Lilian nudged him. "It's your turn…"

"Lilian."

The little girl didn't know what it was exactly. But something about her uncle's tone made her uneasy.

"Did you go out into the Empire on your own?"

"I…" She fidgeted, knowing she was in trouble now. "I just wanted to go with the older kids…they were gonna leave me behind…"

Liam turned his head, catching her with his bright, silver eyes. "What did I tell you about leaving the valley?"

She hid in her blanket.

Reaching out, Liam gently tugged the blanket down just an inch, forcing her to look at him. "Lil. Tell me what I said."

"It…it's dangerous," she answered, repeating his words to her from so long ago, "and I shouldn't go out there, because that's where the Empire is…"

"So why did you disobey?"

"Because…I wanted to see Mekial be an aetheriest, too…" She hiccuped into her blanket.

Liam looked away for a second. "Lilian, what do you think could've happened if we weren't able to make it to you?"

"I don't know…"

"You could've been hurt. Badly."

She sniffed.

"Lil, I need to be able to trust that you'll listen to me."

"I'm sorry…I won't do it again, I promise…"

Liam's gaze shifted over to Greta, who was sound asleep.

He sighed. "We're gonna finish this in the morning."

Lilian sniffled and started to cry softly.

Liam rubbed his face with both hands, tired.

"U-Uncle…" Lilian begged after a space of weeping, "c-can I still hear a story? Please?"

Liam sighed, thinking. At long last he set the lamp down near her head and opened his arms for her. "Come here."

Her eyes wet and cheeks red, Lilian crawled out from under her blankets and curled up in his lap.

Liam was quiet for a moment. "Your mom really hated bugs. Did you know that?"

Sniffing, Lilian shook her head.

So, Liam proceeded to tell her about how Laura had gone out with the gatherers, and had spotted a beetle in her basket the size of a small bird. She'd screamed so shrilly that every other Avat in the group — including him — had nearly gone deaf. No one else had seen the insect and so they'd watched in confusion as Laura had danced and flailed around her basket like she was performing a ritual.

He imitated some of it for Lilian to visualize, making her laugh out loud.

Greta stirred and mumbled something in her sleep.

Liam froze.

Greta smacked her lips. But she didn't wake up.

Sharing looks, he and Lilian snickered softly.

Laura had kicked the basket by accident, Liam continued, and the impressive bug had landed in her hair. By then, everyone had figured out what was going on and he'd snatched the beetle and thrown it back into the woods. It sprouted wings and flew away, he finished, but not before spiraling around Laura as if to tease her. She'd been so hysterical by that point that she'd actually sprinted back home.

"Laura was embarrassed," he finished fondly. "She said she hoped you'd be better with bugs than she was."

Lilian grinned sleepily. "I like bugs."

He smiled back. "Well…she'd be proud."

Lilian's lazy expression remained, even as her eyes began to fall shut.

Liam pushed some hair out of her face. "Night, Lil."

"Good night…" She seemed to drift off, her fearful mind having finally wound down after hearing Liam's tale. But a second later she frowned, her sharp ears alerting her to something outside.

Liam had already heard it: the gentle patter of booted feet hastening across the dirt paths.

"Someone's being noisy outside…" she mumbled.

"I know," he said. Laying her on her mat, he tucked her in. "Try to sleep anyway."

"Are you gonna go see what they're doing?"

"I might."

"Okay…" She rolled onto her side, her brown face caught in the lamplight's flickering glow. "Be careful…Uncle…"

She fell asleep.

Liam picked up the lantern and stood. Scowling towards the window, he turned it off.

He was outside in a second, and instantly caught the sound of voices farther away. They were coming from the farmlands.

"How long before we're s'posed to leave?" he heard one man say.

"Tomorrow night, provided all goes as planned," was the response.

Without a sound, Liam crept along the outer wall of the hut. When he reached a corner, he stopped and squinted around it. A small group of people was gathered at the foot of the main road.

He listened to them closely. If he wasn't mistaken, they were the missing scouts that had returned only just that day.

"We're to grab our horses and rendezvous in the woods, not far from the falls." It was Aizen talking. "The next operation'll commence after that."

"What if the chief finds out?" a woman asked.

A pause. "He'll thank us later. We can't just wait around for the Empire to make the next move."

Something slid across the ground behind Liam. Were he not a Northern Avat, he was sure he would've missed it.

Someone was coming for him.

It was another scout — Kyrah — but by the time she rounded to the side of the hut where she thought she'd seen a loitering silhouette, there was no one there.

She lowered her lifted hands. The light within her palms died.

"Sorry I'm late," she said upon reaching the others. "I thought I saw someone watching you."

"Was anyone there?" one of her allies inquired.

"No. I must've imagined it."

Aizen flipped his eyes to the village.

No sound was leaving it. Not even a shadow moved.

It made sense. By now, everyone in the village was asleep.

"Let's move now, before the next person you see isn't your imagination." He started for the edge of the crop fields, his sights set on the enclosure that hemmed in Taranis' horses and saigas. Like the rest of the village the creatures were asleep, their bodies curled atop the soft grass and their manes shifting in the cool night air. "We'll make it there before Lemm. Izma agreed to wait behind with him, so she'll be able to let him out of the valley."

Neither he nor anyone with him said anything else. They simply marched for the pens and hopped the fences, after which they gently nudged some of the horses awake.

Recognizing the faces that had neared them, the beasts clambered upright and allowed the group to saddle them up. Once they were equipped for their journey the entire party rode away, leaping over the fences that had once walled them in to gallop into the darkness beyond.

None of them looked back.

So none of them saw Liam creep over the crest of Greta's roof and perch atop it, his stony face as still as his stony form.

Brent's head was bowed in thought when he arrived at Adelle's gravesite. When he raised his eyes, he stopped short upon seeing who was there.

Hearing his approach, Lemm turned from the tree to see him.

A strange smile split his face. "Takin' a stroll, kid?"

69

I TAKE IT YOU couldn't sleep." Lemm's eyes were unblinking, but his countenance displayed no real interest in Brent's insomnia.

Brent shifted his weight. At length, he shook his head.

"One of your scouts told me that this is where they buried her." Turning, Lemm looked at the curvy script that had been carved into Adelle's headstone. "It's funny. She'd always talk about this hill whenever I went to visit her. She'd light up when she did. Guess I can see why." He peered into the valley. With the amari tree being settled upon a hill that wound higher than the village, he could see the field in all of its entirety. Even the lake was visible. "Not a bad view."

Brent said nothing.

"I heard a lot about you from your fellow villagers." Lemm looked at him, transitioning into the next topic as if it were as natural as breathing. "You've been makin' quite the name for yourself since I brought you here."

Brent cut his eyes at him. "Left me here, you mean."

Lemm didn't reply to that.

Brent didn't drag it out. He tilted his gaze aside with a sharp pinch of his brow.

Lemm looked him over shortly. "That hardly looks like the face of someone who's been outsmarting slave traders for the past year. I hear they even gave you a nickname. Skylok, am I right?"

Brent pursed his lips. He didn't think he could ignore the obvious for very much longer.

"I never expected any apologies from you," he said. "But…I owe you one." His vision fell to the grave and it lingered there for a second. "…I'm sorry. If I could change how things turned out that day…I would."

Lemm eyed him with a raised eyebrow before turning back to Adelle's grave. "Wasn't your fault, kid. But I guess it was me who told you that it was, huh? And you're right." A sharp wind tousled his messy pompadour. He looked strangely pensive. "I did leave you. All of you."

A moment passed before he continued. "My cousin always put the lives of others ahead of her own, to the very end. Can't really be mad at her for it. She lived the way she wanted." He smiled bitterly. "Whenever she met a runaway Avat, she'd move heaven and earth to get them to safety. Even I couldn't keep myself from helping her out, whenever I could. She was so passionate about it. And discreet enough to never get caught." He stood straighter. "So when she sent you my way she probably figured I'd do something, even though I'd told her I was gonna quit.

"And then the Empire got her. The noble and generous Adelle…killed by a poisoned arrow. She must've been in so much pain."

Brent held his silence.

"Still, in the end, it seems like her sacrifice wasn't a waste." Lemm circled to look at Brent once more. "I hear Taranis is the biggest Liberation Front thanks to you. Can't say I've ever had the pleasure of visiting any of the other ones myself but, I'm willin' to take people's word for it."

"Yeah…" Brent's eyes shifted to the side once more. "I've heard the same. Things have been going well here, for a while. Until today."

"Yep. Nothin' kills complacency like a wildfire ragin' on your doorstep." Lemm smiled absently. It hardly hid the contempt that he felt.

"…Yeah." Brent suddenly felt worn out.

For the longest time, he'd believed that the auction raids he'd been leading had been chipping away at the slave trade.

But they weren't. The truth was that one by one, the Liberation Fronts were being picked off. Taranis had nearly been next.

The crippling truth of what that meant burdened him: that no matter how much they seemed to progress here, in this village on the edge of the world, the horrors of the slave trade and the Empire's tyranny ran rampant everywhere else. Indeed, they were only right next door.

The reality of it all made him feel foolish.

All he'd ever wanted was to give slaves the chance to have a home like the one Adelle had died to give him. All he'd ever hoped for was that they'd be able to live in peace just as he had for the last seven years, away from the corruption, the hatred, the enslavement. He thought he'd finally been attaining that goal but now, with a month-long hiatus and one invasion attempt, he felt as if he'd pla-teaued.

Was there nothing else he could do to help the people he so des-perately wanted to save? Was there really nothing more, aside from raiding slave auctions and retreating back here, that he could do to make sure that everyone and anyone who suffered at the hands of the Empire could live the lives that they deserved? Would they never be able to change anything in the Arkanian Empire?

He stopped, startled by the implications of his own ambition.

Change the Empire.

Was that what he wanted?

Was that what would fix everything?

But how would he even go about it? The Empire was vast, with a fixed system that dated back centuries.

Still, if nothing changed, then his fight alongside the Liberation Fronts wouldn't get any easier. And then, eventually, every sanctuary village that still existed would be snuffed out, and their names and battles would be wiped from the annals of history.

He didn't want that. It made the hope that the Liberation Fronts offered a fleeting and meaningless one.

Avats, and the people who supported them, needed more than that.

"I wonder what'd happen if you guys retaliated against the

Empire for this," Lemm said suddenly and Brent was torn from his gloomy thoughts. "If this is how much Taranis has changed after adding one new kid to its ranks, I wonder what'd happen if you switched up your tactics and avenged yourselves."

He shifted to look at Brent, a gleam in his eye. "That's what you've been having this place do anyway, right? How else would Taranis manage to swell to the size it's gotten, unless someone changed its methods of operation?"

Brent blinked, startled.

"If I know the chief," Lemm went on, "he'll resort to what he knows best, and will have the village stand down. Cease all raids, all intelligence scouting, just in case the release of more fighters will stir up the Empire's interest in this region again. But I'd wager that that's because he's thinkin' too small. He's still caught up in the ways of Taranis' founding."

"He'd be trying to protect us," Brent pointed out with a frown.

"Yeah." Lemm rubbed the back of his neck. He looked sorely uninterested in Brent's defensive statement. "Be a prudent leader and all that, right? Guess that works, y'know, when you've got time for it."

"What's that supposed to mean?"

"Exactly what I said." Lemm dropped his hand. "You really think the Empire's not gonna come back to finish what it started? Especially once word gets out that every man they sent in didn't report back. They can't even recover the bodies. That's bound to arouse suspicion."

Brent clenched his jaw and tore his eyes away.

"You seem like a smart kid." Lemm tilted his head with an eerie smile. "And I've got an idea."

Brent dared to meet his eye. "What is it?"

"Just a thought on how Taranis could defend itself. And what you could do to help."

Brent hesitated. But he wanted to know more.

"Tell you what," Lemm read the interest on his face. "The chief likes to work fast. By this time tomorrow, he'll have made a decision on what Taranis should do next. If you think he's got a good plan, then go ahead and support him. But if it's an order for you to stand your ground and wait it out, meet me near that barrier of yours for an alternative. If you're not there by moonrise, I'll know what choice you made."

Brent paused, considering.

"It's your call. But I doubt someone like you would take too kindly to twiddling his thumbs. Feel free to think it over," he added, spying Brent's scowl of hesitation, and he started for the trees.

"…You never planned to stay for long, did you?" Brent asked as Lemm walked past him.

Lemm chuckled. "No. Actually, I think I might've overstayed my welcome already."

Though Brent quirked an eyebrow in confusion, Lemm didn't explain himself. He simply continued back to the village.

Brent frowned after him, nightly winds coursing over the hilltop to breeze through his hair. When the moonlight glanced off of Lemm's mask, a certain memory touched his mind.

"…A few weeks ago," he began and at the utterance of his words, Lemm stopped and turned his head a bit, "during the last Feast of Liberty, I came up here." He paused for a moment. "I… used to visit her often."

Lemm held his peace, waiting with a calmness that almost seemed unnatural.

"I thought I saw someone here that day," Brent went on, his eyes falling to Lemm's mask again. "Someone who was wearing a mask just like yours."

Lemm's cobalt stare moved to the trees where they settled on nothing, distant.

While the mere thought of voicing his next query seemed foolish, Brent plowed ahead anyway. "Was it you?"

Lemm lifted an eyebrow, intrigued. He shrugged. "Ain't been here in seven years, kid."

Brent's scowl hardened.

He'd wanted to ask if Lemm had been the one to end the wildfires, too. But, so far as he knew, Lemm wasn't an aetheriest.

That probably hadn't been him, either.

"What is it, anyway?" he pressed, choosing a different topic to move on to. "That mask. Back when you found me, and decided to help me save Adelle, I saw it in one of your rooms. On top of that," he cut his eyes at him, "someone else mentioned a name that sounds like yours: Çaru'qu. He said…that 'Çaru'qu doesn't make mistakes'. And that he's picked someone to fight some kind of crisis that's brewing in Arkania. Something worse than everything we fight against." He didn't dare elaborate on who the person had said that Çaru'qu had chosen. "You know anything about that?"

Lemm snickered, and soon the gentle noise built into a full-blown laugh. Though it was full of mirth, it was also touched by a darkness that no hand could grasp.

Brent simply stared at him, baffled.

"Looks like he was right," Lemm said at last, a smile lingering on his lips, and his twinkling eyes landed on Brent. "No one in the Empire really knows the story." He chuckled again, more so at himself, and his gaze fell introspectively. "Then again…I didn't know much myself."

Frowning, Brent opened his mouth again.

"We'll have to save story time for another night, kid," Lemm simpered. "I think I'll rest my tired self up for tomorrow. Maybe you can use that curiosity of yours as an incentive, for when you make your decision."

Brent closed his mouth.

Without another word Lemm vanished into the darkness of the dancing trees and the whispers of nightly wind, leaving Brent to ponder their interaction, and Lemm's offer, in silence.

✶

Koberius' goblet clattered to the floor when he dropped it. Scarlet wine gushed out of it like a leaking wound.

Sweating and huffing painfully, he seized his left eye. Spools of his indigo-blue hair fell around his face, walling off his flushed cheeks, and he seized the edge of the dining table to retain his balance. Spanning almost the entire length of the palace dining hall, it was partially dressed with platters of steaming food. He'd barely touched any of it before his eye had begun to burn him.

At his side, Foedia stretched her hands towards him. The dim torchlight caught the rough texture of her skin. "Your Majesty!"

Still gripping his face, Koberius slapped her arm away.

She backed away with a pale yelp.

"Don't…touch me," he snarled. Bone showed through the skin of his hand as he pressed his palm into his eye. His very breathing started to sound like a growl.

The torches along the wall flickered as the pressure around him changed. Even some of the dishes on the table began to compress, as if something was slowly sitting on it.

Koberius continued to pant quietly, angrily.

Along the red-columned walls, the guards stationed to watch over him glanced about anxiously.

All at once, the doors nearest to the emperor's seat slammed open and a messenger barreled inside.

"Your Highness!" he exclaimed and then, coming to himself right when the guards moved to subdue him, he dropped to kowtow before the ruler.

"His Imperial Majesty is eating right now." Foedia circled to the other side of Koberius to stand between him and the messenger. "Whatever it is, it can wait."

"Lady Foedia!" The messenger lifted his head to see her. "I understand, but, it's urgent! Katruskik rebels have closed in on Prinia! They slipped through the blockade of Empyrean's Guard that were stationed along the Brusseir-Lenora border, and they have the entire shrine city under siege! If we don't help them, the priests and the Temple of Empyrean could be in danger!"

Koberius' breathing finally leveled out. "Let them have it."

Foedia turned on Koberius, putting the imperial ruler in the messenger's line of sight.

"H-Highness?" The messenger stared at him in disbelief.

Behind his curtain of hair, Koberius smiled. "Yes…Prinia." He lifted his head slightly, and his golden eyes seemed to glow. The slitted pupil of his left eye peeked through his fingers, its black depths lit by the angry red mark that hovered inside of it. "That will do just perfectly."

The room in the apartment that Lemm had taken was rather plain, with a sleeping mat fixed in a corner, a few thin blankets, and a window that looked out into the farmlands. The sky stretched wide above it, stars twinkling among the galaxies, and soft moonbeams crossed the vale to creep over the windowsill.

Closing the door, Lemm crossed over to that window. He moved at an amble, and upon reaching the sill he looked out into the night, acting like he was considering the stars.

"You just gonna hang around in the shadows all night?" he asked, folding his arms. "Can't say I enjoy the thought of a guy watching me while I sleep."

The gentle patting of footsteps came from behind him and a black silhouette separated from the darkness to stand in the light.

"I wasn't hiding," Oruviçu said calmly.

"Heh. Obviously not." Lemm turned around and the moonlight gave his cobalt eyes a cool, otherworldly shine. "I've learned that you're really only seen when you wanna be."

Reaching up, Oruviçu removed his mask to reveal his own glowing stare.

"So?" Lemm cocked an eyebrow. "Don't tell me you're actually following me around now."

"Taranis has been getting rather popular, it would seem," Oruviçu replied plainly. "I didn't expect to run into you here."

"So you just happened to have business here then? That's convenient."

"Likewise." Somehow, Oruviçu's calm, unblinking stare reminded Lemm of a cat. "Or perhaps it's fate."

Lemm scoffed. "Well, in that case, what now? Gonna try and save me from myself again?" He leaned against the window nonchalantly, elbows up to rest on the sill. He cocked his head with a conceited little grin. "Think we both know how that's gonna end."

"I'm known for being stubborn." Oruviçu hooked his mask to a bit on his shoulder and with a light touch of his mind, he caused the braided mane attached to it to slither around his neck like a fur mantle. "Something your cousin often pointed out."

"I'm also stubborn." Lemm's face hardened like steel: his smile dropped, his eyebrows furrowed. His displeasure was obvious. "Just cuz you and Adelle once had a thing goin' doesn't give you the right to butt in on my affairs. I told you that already."

"Perhaps so." Oruviçu's bright eyes turned to Lemm's mask, which was currently hooked to his shoulder. "But I can't simply abandon you. After all," his gaze shifted to Lemm's, "I am partly to blame for all you're now involved in. You…and Ivan."

Lemm laughed dryly. "Great. So you're helping me to ease your own conscience. How typical of the great Commander Orvis: always looking to make amends after he's the one who made the blunders that needed 'em."

Oruviçu was quiet. His face betrayed no emotion.

"Let it go, *Orvie.*" Lemm shifted to make himself more comfortable, smirking. "I'm only joking. Sort of."

"Every man makes mistakes, and every man has regrets," Oruviçu said. "I'm only trying to keep you from making one that you may regret for the rest of your life."

"What, scared I might end up like you? Please. Think I've got more brains than that."

"If that's true, what is this I've heard about your plans for the boy that Ivan took in?"

Lemm's face darkened. "You spyin' on me, Orvis?"

"If I have been, you would know why." Oruviçu wasn't put off by Lemm's threatening look. "Due to his blood…the boy's affairs are mine."

Lemm huffed. "As dutiful and stiff as ever. No clue what Adelle saw in you."

Oruviçu was again stiff-faced, completely unreadable. But then his eyes fell as he actually mulled it over. "…Heart," he said at last.

"'Scuse me?"

"Adelle always saw one's heart first." Oruviçu looked him over. "She did the same with you. That's why she trusted you so much."

Lemm just looked at him blackly. Then, all at once, his shoulders jumped with a snicker that slowly ascended into a chuckle. "Sorry," he said at last, when he'd gain the will to control himself.

"It's just that that sounds rich. Coming from you."

"I advise that you end this, Lemm," Oruviçu said evenly. "Mark me: you have no idea what you're facilitating. Or what your bloodshed is allowing."

"I'm only ending the lives of the kinds of people that made Adelle's life difficult," Lemm cut in sharply. "And mine. And Ivan's. How else do people think this fight that the Liberation Fronts are in is gonna end? With a pompous ceremony and leaders gathered around a table, shaking hands? Don't make me laugh." He straightened up. "This is efficiency. And this" — he tapped the ferocious mask that was hooked to his shoulder — "is the only face that'll make them take it seriously. Poetic, isn't it?" He smiled vainly, his hand lowering. "It's like that story you told me is finally starting to come full circle."

Oruviçu stared at him, hard, with those glowing eyes of his, as if he was making a book's worth of calculations in under a few seconds.

"Well? Still gonna try and stop me?" Lemm dared.

"…I see."

"You see what?" Lemm actually frowned.

"Every man makes mistakes, and every man has regrets," the Avat said once more. "And every man must own the choices that he makes."

Lemm stared at him, his jaw clenching and unclenching. "Take it that means you'll let it go."

"I will." Oruviçu slowly retreated into the shadows once more. "And I hope you do the same…before it's too late."

Lemm looked aside with a short flash of his teeth.

When he looked across the room again, Oruviçu was gone.

70

A VIOLENT COUGHING FIT overtook Diomedes' lungs, forcing him against a wall while he was only halfway down the corridor. With his shoulders hunching, he pressed his handkerchief against his mouth.

"Father!" Having been passing by with Mattatheus at her side, Adiné hurried to help him. "Are you all right?!"

Diomedes couldn't answer through his coughing.

Adiné looked to Mattatheus. "Get the doctor!"

He nodded shortly and disappeared around the corner with a billow of his cape.

At his back Adiné held onto her father, offering her support in the best way that she could.

It seemed that he'd always been like this, she thought, succumbing to fits of coughing and wheezing at the most abrupt of times. She supposed if she considered it, it had all started when she was around nine years old. That had been when he'd taken her on her first tour of the province.

Their trip had ended suddenly after visiting Peluma, and to this day Adiné still didn't know why. She only knew that ever since then, her father's health had begun to deteriorate.

"Adiné," Diomedes managed, breaking her thoughts. He peered up at her weakly, having not realized she was there with him. "You should…be at your aether training…"

"Not until you're better." Helping him to stand, she escorted him into a small sitting room.

Since they were on the second level of the estate it had a balcony that looked out over the manor's western lawn, with its trimmed hedges and rolling field, and the pediments and columns of Axelius spotted the skyline. The room itself was ornamented with a mosaic floor and painted walls, as well as padded seating that encircled a low table.

Adiné led Diomedes to one of the chairs and had him recline in it.

He coughed for a minute longer. "Th…thank you…"

She smiled faintly, a hand on his back.

A second later, Mattatheus arrived with the estate physician in tow.

Seeing the viceroy, the woman went to him. She spoke a few words to him, to which he nodded with a very hoarse response.

Hardly a second later, he succumbed to another horrible fit. At its completion, he lowered his handkerchief.

On it, there was a splotch of blood the size of his palm.

Subtle concern arose on Mattatheus' face. He stepped forward but, not knowing what he could do, he didn't move any closer.

Again, Diomedes surrendered to another tide of coughing, and the physician quickly sifted through her supplies for something to use as treatment.

Spiraling, Adiné swiftly left the room.

Mattatheus glanced between her and the viceroy. Then, choosing to leave the provincial leader to the medical expert, he went after the princess.

He found her not even a few corridors away, standing in an alcove with her hands clasped together. A statue of Vedrah was in front of her and on her left and right, there were open archways that led to a small, verdant courtyard. The sound of fountain water could be heard bubbling within.

Adiné's eyes were closed, and her thin eyebrows were crinkled with distress. She didn't notice Mattatheus at all.

Wanting to keep it that way, he lingered behind a potted plant, out of sight.

"Please," he heard her beg softly, "Vedrah, god of life waters…"

When she opened her eyes, tears slid down her smooth, even cheeks. "Please…don't take my father from me, too."

Clamping her eyes shut again, she clasped her hands tighter and bowed her head once more.

Mattatheus turned aside. Without a sound, he circled around the nearest corner, leaving the princess to her privacy.

"Kurt really likes this stuff." As evening's light bathed all of Taranis, Lilian smiled at the fresh bread that was set in the baker's window. "He says it's like eating a cloud."

Bending down, Liam looked into the window with her.

The bakery, which also doubled as the baker's house, stood along the road that faced the farmlands. Villagers walked to and fro in front of it, but some did slip inside to pick up a loaf for home.

Liam and Lilian were there to do the same, with Lilian having made a special order for Kurt. With classes now over and the day coming to an end, she meant to bring it to him.

In every sense, it looked like a regular day in Taranis. But a vaporous mist of unease crept at everyone's feet, birthed after the events of the fire from the day previous.

As far as Liam was aware, no one knew how close the village had actually come to being destroyed. The only ones who did know had sworn themselves to secrecy, himself included.

He'd instructed Lilian to say nothing of it as well. From what she'd shared with him when he'd picked her up from class, her friends were being just as quiet.

"Hey, Uncle Liam?" she looked at him.

"Hm?"

"Um…are you okay?"

He stood up fully. "What do you mean?"

"Well," the little girl glanced away, "while I was at school, I looked out the window and I saw you were talking to Kro. You looked really mad."

Liam didn't see any reason to hide it. "I was. Because he put you and your friends in danger."

"Oh…"

"Here you go!" An Avat woman emerged from the bakery with Lilian's order in hand: a bread roll twisted into a pretzel. It seemed to be mixed with sweet corn. "I had it cooling off for a bit but it's still hot, so be careful!"

"Thank you, Henrietta!" Lilian extended her arms for her handwoven bag and clutched it to her chest. She inhaled. "It smells great!"

"Only the best for our little Lilian and friends." Henrietta slipped Liam a kind wink.

He smiled softly.

"Is there jam?" Lilian gasped. "I forgot, I want some of that, too!"

Henrietta's brown face glowed as she laughed. "You know we've always got jam, Lilian! But to tell the truth, I didn't make it this time. We've got someone new helping us out now and they wanted to try their hand at it."

"Aw…" Lilian seemed disappointed. "So it won't taste the same?"

"Henrietta's got everyone who's working with her following the same recipes, Lil," Liam told her. "It shouldn't taste any different."

"Really?"

"That's right!" Henrietta assured her. "Everyone here follows the same recipes with all the right proportions. And every jar of jam is personally approved by me!"

"Wow, really?"

"Of course!"

Liam smiled gently at the sight of his niece's excitement. But a glint of movement in the corner of his eye soon drew his attention away from her.

A young man had approached the window that was on the other side of the bakery door. Bending at the knee, he peeked inside to look at the bread basket that was on display.

He seemed troubled.

Squinting, Liam soon recognized him. If he wasn't mistaken, he'd been a part of Aizen and Kyrah's rotation.

Did that mean the scouts had decided to return?

Ignorant of Liam's watchful eye, the villager righted himself. He didn't seem to want bread anymore, for he walked away without going inside.

"Do you have any prune jam?" Lilian suddenly exclaimed.

Liam wheeled around, his calm face actually breaking with surprise. "Wait, Lil —!"

"I think I've got a couple of leftovers," Henrietta recalled. "I'll go grab you some now!"

She vanished inside and Liam sighed defeatedly.

After just a taste of that jam, his niece would be on a sugar rush for the entire night. He'd never get any sleep.

"Liam."

He turned.

Another villager was coming towards him and when he got close enough for Liam to see, he learned that it was Chief Ivan's assistant.

"Yuan," he greeted and he figured out what the man likely wanted. "Is the chief ready to tell us what's next?"

Lilian looked up curiously.

"Yes," Yuan responded, his grim, black eyes alight with the glow of sunset. "The meeting is going to be in the dining hall of the Main House. All raiders and scouts are required to attend."

"When?"

"Now."

～ � ～

Ivan wanted everyone to stand down, just like Lemm had predicted.

He didn't go into any details. But he did imply that Taranis was in a precarious situation, and that if they continued to conduct raids and scouting missions, there was a chance they would alert the

Empire of their location.

So, until further notice, there would be a curfew, an increased night watch that would expand posts into the valley, and there would be no more assignments.

When Brent heard the order, his disappointment was plain. As the chief departed the hall and ascended to the second floor conference room, he wallowed in his discouragement for a moment.

"I'm gonna turn in," he said finally, his words for Aaron, Renée and Liam, who'd sat with him during the announcement. Without waiting for any of them to respond, he filed out of the hall with several others.

"Y'know…he's been acting strange all day," Renée observed.

"I noticed," Aaron agreed darkly.

Arms folded and his ankle crossed over his knee, Liam said nothing.

"Hey, I heard something earlier." Renée turned from the dispersing villagers to face the two of them. "The scouts are missing again."

"What?" Aaron frowned. "Where'd you hear that?"

"Not long before I came in. Someone said he saw them come to the Main House for a debriefing with the chief late last night. But after that, no one's seen any sign of them."

Aaron was in disbelief.

"She's right," Liam said.

They faced him.

"The scouts left. Late." He stood up.

Aaron stared at him, bug-eyed.

"Aizen and Kyrah were with them," Liam went on. "Whatever they're up to, they don't want the chief or anyone else to find out."

"Did you overhear anything they said?" Aaron asked, managing to compose himself.

"Just something about a meeting with Lemm and an operation beginning tonight."

Aaron knit his brow.

Renée was just as quizzical.

"Ren!"

She turned around, her eyes jumping to the Main House's

entrance.

Mekial was there, forcing his way through the last of the villagers that were leaving. When he made it inside, he stopped short. "Wait, is the meeting over?!"

"Yeah." She frowned. "Why, did you wanna come? Trainees aren't allowed in, remember?"

"Yeah, yeah, I know…" He made his way towards her and cast the room a disheartened look. "Man, I wish I'd gotten here in time!"

"Why'd you want to sit in on the meeting?"

"Because I had some really important intel to share!" Mekial burst, rounding on her with wide, excited eyes. He lowered his voice and spoke behind the back of his hand. "It was about what happened yesterday. I'm sure the chief would've needed to hear it, but I got it handed to me by Jeffrey and Miss Yulia for missing both of their lessons yesterday." He dropped his hand. "Jeffrey made me run like, thirty laps around the village, including the farmlands, and Miss Yulia made me do a whole exercise on why I shouldn't skip classes. It took all day! I couldn't even visit Kurt! I would've told you about it last night," he prattled on, "but I was so tired when I got back, and when I woke up you weren't home."

"Yesterday?" Aaron repeated. "While you were in Odelwhite?"

"Yeah." Mekial faced him. "Me, Lilian and the others overheard the guardsmen talking about some weird stuff that's been happening in the Empire."

Aaron's piercing eyes narrowed. "Weird how?"

"They said that the auction raiders have been killing a bunch of people over the past month. The way they were talking about it, it sounded like that was why they were in the forest to find Taranis at all. They even made it sound like the people who died had been murdered. But whoever was doing it, I don't think they were rescuing slaves at the same time."

"We would've received a message to escort them here if anyone *was* sending slaves back this way," Renée pointed out. "Are you sure you heard them say that?"

"Pretty sure."

"We haven't dispatched anyone over the past month," Aaron

murmured, his bright eyes on the floor.

"That's what I said!" Mekial cried.

"So, someone's been killing imperials and giving us the credit for it?" Renée summarized. She looked at Aaron, who was still scowling at the floor in contemplation.

"…Ren," he said at last, "take Mekial to my dad. He should hear this."

"I can go by myself!" Mekial protested. "I don't need a babysitter."

Aaron rubbed his temple irritably. "It's not about being babysat, Mekial. Dad's probably in another meeting with the head council upstairs. Yuan will be outside, but he won't let just anyone in to talk to the chief."

"Then I'll just tell him you sent me! Even Yuan can't ignore an order from the chief's son, right?"

Aaron looked at Renée.

She shrugged.

"Fine," he agreed. "Go, now."

Nodding, Mekial hurried to the upper floor.

"Okay then." Renée faced Liam and Aaron completely, hands on her hips. "What now?"

Aaron thought for a second. "The scouts may be gone," he started, "but I think that Lemm guy might know something, since he's the one they're doing this secret mission with. We've been living under a rock for the past month. We oughta know what's going on outside our walls. I don't know if he's still in the apartments, given what Liam saw, but it's all we've got to go on right now."

"I'll go with you," Liam said.

"Is Lemm the same guy who saved Mekial and the others? He was the one in that mask, right?" Renée asked.

"Yeah," Aaron confirmed. "Apparently he's an old friend of Taranis. Both my parents know him as Adelle's cousin."

Renée was taken aback by that. But she still nodded her understanding. "Okay. Then I'm coming, too. With the chief's stand-down order in place, I'm still barred from regular missions. I'm not about to let my training go to waste."

Aaron nodded grimly. "Let's go then."*tv*

ONE TRICK PONY
CODE: STANDDOWN

Outside, the trio navigated the emptying, nightly roads and soon came to the apartment that Lemm had been guided to. Granted directions by a tenant, they came to the room that he'd taken.

It was empty.

Aaron took one step inside, scanning the bare walls and open window as if there was some secret hiding place for Lemm to have tucked himself away in.

Upon hearing someone coming down the hall, he stepped back out in two strides.

The villager crashed into him, startled by his abrupt appearance, and he held her by the arms to keep her steady.

"Aaron!" the Avat exclaimed.

"Sorry," he said quickly. "Do you know where the guy who was staying in this room went?"

"He left early this morning," the young woman recalled after a short time of thought. "He didn't say much. He just went upstairs to eat and left. I haven't seen him since."

Aaron frowned, his absent gaze wandering away as he tried to consider where Lemm could've possibly taken off to. He shared a questioning look with Renée.

Behind them, Liam walked away.

Aaron frowned. "Where're you going?"

Liam spoke over his shoulder as he marched out. "To find someone else who can help."

✧ ✼ ✧

Orion yawned loudly as he crossed the lobby of the northern apartments. It was a dark place given the time of night and what with the near-silence of the connecting halls, it almost seemed like he was walking through an abandoned building.

He thought nothing of it however, far too preoccupied with the abrupt urge to relieve himself, which had struck him while he'd been in his room.

His soft, animal-hide shoes barely made a sound against the

wooden floor and when he reached the door, he pulled it agape. With the other, he scratched one of his pointy ears.

He jumped half a foot when he saw Aaron, Renée and Liam on the threshold.

None of them looked the least bit happy.

Aaron's vivid eyes were the only things that moved: they looked Orion up and down sharply. "This him?"

"Yeah," Liam said.

"Well, at least we didn't have to look too hard."

Orion gawked and teetered with surprise when Aaron gripped him by the shoulder and walked him back inside.

Liam and Renée trekked in after them, the door closing in their wake, and they ventured to the center of the lobby.

Liam tipped his head at a slight angle and listened to the halls.

It didn't sound like anyone was coming.

Tilting to see Aaron, he flicked his chin down.

Aaron circled to the young, wide-eyed villager. "Sorry if this is unexpected," he began, "but we need your help with something."

"No," Orion shook his head calmly after Aaron's explanation of the reason for their visit. "I'm not one of the scouts from the last rotation. I'm not with any of the scouts at all." He hastily added another statement when Aaron exchanged a silent look with Liam. "But, my brother Evan is a scout. He's my twin."

Aaron revolved to face him. "Your twin."

Orion nodded speedily.

Aaron blinked at him. He was just noticing the irony of the situation but with that wordless scowl on his face, his stormy look was chilling.

Orion, shorter than him with boyish features that were even more youthful than Aaron's and of an age that was just a couple of years younger than the chief's eldest, swallowed softly.

Aaron took a step back. "So…who are you?"

For some reason, that made Orion feel less important. He answered him anyway. "Orion. My brother and I were rescued in a raid a few months ago, right before an auctioneer could separate us by selling my brother away. I help out in the farmlands."

"I guess I was mistaken," Liam noted, briefly earning Orion's eye. "So your brother is with them."

"We'll work with it." Aaron accepted the change in circumstance. "If you're at least related to one of the scouts, then you can probably tell us where he is. The chief had us all come in for a meeting today but as far as we could tell, your brother and all of the scouts from his rotation weren't around for it. Did he tell you anything?"

Orion's eyes darted from him to Liam, whose silver stare was more daunting than Aaron's. If he didn't know any better he would've believed the blonde Avat to be blind, but his reputation as one of Taranis' best warriors had already told him otherwise. Truthfully, it made his gaze that much more impactful.

Aaron held a different kind of authority, he thought next. The young raider, who also doubled as an incredible reconnaissance scout, hadn't even reached the age of twenty but seemed to carry a presence that was on its way to bearing as much weight as his father. Indeed, standing before him was like standing before a much younger version of Chief Ivan himself.

Then, there was Renée. Far more beautiful in person, he'd heard plenty about her from his friends who were in training at the sparring hall. Her kind face was unassuming, for she apparently had the skill to do battle with men twice her size, and win. It was said that she'd been enrolled in Jeffrey's private tutoring sessions, along with Brent, Aaron and Liam. He certainly didn't want to cross her.

Orion had never met any of them before, though he admittedly hadn't been living in Taranis for very long. He could only wonder why any of them needed to talk to him specifically about the issue they'd brought up.

Then again, he probably did have information that not even they, in their esteemed ranks in Taranis' forces, had access to.

"Yeah…" His eyes fell sadly. "He did mention something to me last night."

"What was it?" Renée asked.

"Well, if he really meant what he was saying, then he and the other scouts from his rotation aren't even in Taranis anymore."

"We figured as much," Aaron replied. "And if they said something about an operation with Lemm, that'd explain why he's gone, too."

"Evan mentioned someone with that name!" Orion exclaimed. "Lemm. He said that Lemm helped him to realize that auction raiding isn't enough in regards to Taranis' mission. They have to 'do more'."

Aaron's eyes narrowed at that paraphrased statement. "Did he happen to say anything about something that happened last month in the Empire?"

"Yeah." Orion seemed surprised at the specificity of Aaron's guess. "He and the other scouts…they've been going on a killing spree."

Aaron's eyes grew large beneath his furrowed brow and he opened his mouth to question him further.

"Ssh!" Liam faced one of the hallways, his hand spread to quiet them. "…Someone's coming."

"We should talk somewhere else," Aaron decided gravely.

"Somewhere with access to a map," Orion added and while Aaron didn't seem to understand the reason for it, he dipped his chin to agree.

Orion smiled nervously. "But, uh…can I go to the outhouse first? I've kinda been holding it in for a while."

Liam eyed him quietly. As per usual, his face couldn't be read.

Renée turned from Liam to Aaron. The calm look on her face showed consent.

Aaron didn't hide his annoyance. But he soon overcame it with a deep sigh. "Fine…"

⭐

The lights in the schoolhouse were out. It was no surprise, for the hour was late.

They hurried to the building shortly after Orion had handled his business. Climbing the outside staircase to reach the front entrance, they passed inside and gathered in its central room, which acted as a lounge space for the children in between lessons.

A map was hanging on one of the far walls. After Liam and Aaron pushed a few of the tables together, Renée and Orion took it down and spread it out on their combined surfaces.

Lighting on one of the oil lamps, Aaron placed it at the edge of the map.

"Evan once told me that he was losing faith in the Liberation Fronts," Orion began and with one hand he flattened the map out. His black eyes inched over to the Province of Lyrik, neighbor to Taranis. "He didn't think Taranis would be able to hold out for much longer, if all it ever did was rescue slaves and retreat to bring them back here. We're immobile. The Empire would find us someday. Then he told me about what happened with the fires yesterday…it almost had."

Aaron, Renée and Liam waited for him to continue.

Orion picked up a stick of charcoal from atop one of the tables and leaned over Lyrik. "Evan didn't think that anyone else thought the way he did until he got placed into the last rotation. He said he and the scout he was paired up with, Kyrah, ran into that man you mentioned, Lemm, in Orinn. They were stationed there. Apparently, Lemm had been causing trouble across the Empire already."

"As Saruke's Shade," Aaron said decidedly. "For the past year. Right?"

Orion nodded.

"Evan said Lemm started off solo. After he'd gotten a reputation murdering nobles out in Nassaul, people started to call him 'Saruke's Shade'. I'm not sure why, and Evan wasn't either, but he knows that people spoke of him like was some kind of apocalyptic omen. No one knew if he was a man or some kind of demon. He seemed to travel faster than possible, and wreak plenty more havoc than most in such short windows of time." Orion marked the towns of Barrae and Revale in the easternmost province, as well as areas in between that likely indicated lesser known villages and hamlets. Moving west, he marked Calig, a small mining town cupped in the mountains of the Eastern Mines, and then marked a couple of places along the southern tip of Zenrikk's Gorge, a terrifying chasm in Lenora that practically split the province in half.

"By the time he reached Cleopa" — Orion marked it — "he'd gotten the attention of mercenaries and outlaws, who decided to join his…revolution." He marked the Southern Mines. "They took out slave traders around here, disrupting mining operations for weeks. They were pretty silent out here in Lyrik, until they attacked Orinn, where Kyrah and Evan met him. They helped him attack Orinn that same night."

Orion marked the town.

"Evan told me that Lemm could understand their frustration," he continued solemnly. "He tapped into our scouts' disillusionment with the Liberation Fronts' actions, and how they felt like they weren't doing enough to really make a difference.

"Eventually, the other scouts caught on to what was happening and I guess, long story short, they all agreed that the true freeing of slaves began with the total annihilation of anyone who justified slavery."

"So that's why they were killing noblemen and slave traders," Renée deduced.

"Not just noblemen. They killed soldiers. Patrolmen. Travelers. Lemm and his original band of allies did most of the killing." Orion made a few more marks between Orinn and the farming village of Gilead to the south. Inching across the parchment, he continued to mark areas along the road leading to Bengai, and worked his way down to Devon, then Ribbosheth, just outside of the Odelwhite Forest. "They also infiltrated the homes of wealthy slave owners here. I don't know how many." He made a mark on top of Peluma. "Do you see a pattern?"

Aaron leaned over the map and studied it.

"It's like…from the beginning," Renée put a finger on Barrae, "he's been working his way towards us. He never went into northern Lenora, or even Brusseir."

"Yeah," Aaron agreed. "His whole route heads through southern Nassaul and cuts straight into Lyrik. After that, all of his attacks happened right outside of Odelwhite."

They looked at each other.

"Right," Orion confirmed. "Evan thinks that the guardsmen

invaded not only because they've been tracking our raiders, but also because of where Lemm's most recent string of attacks have been."

"They wanted to catch two birds with one stone," Liam determined. "The Empire was already looking into our location, since they see us as a threat. Lemm's just as dangerous. They probably thought we were allies and decided to move in. Catch us all together."

"What about the slaves?" Aaron asked, leaning against the table and staring at the markings. "Since the Liberation Front of Uboris was found by Empyrean's Guard up in the Adriak Mountains, Taranis has become the only sanctuary village around any of these sites for miles. If they were gonna send them anywhere, it would've been here. But as far as any of us know, we haven't gotten any requests to ferry anyone in. Where'd they put them?"

Orion hesitated.

"Where'd they put them?" Aaron repeated, punching out every word.

Orion shook his head. "I-I don't know. Evan doesn't, either. But, he had an idea…"

"What?"

"Maybe some of them managed to escape to other sister villages in the neighboring provinces. But that's unlikely. And if they were recaptured, the Empire probably didn't sell them back into slavery. Instead, they probably gave them to the priests as sacrifices. Evan did say once that the emperor's been increasing the demand for them…"

Renée looked to be on the verge of being sick.

Aaron's eyes widened in alarm. "And our scouts have been okay with that?!"

"It's not his fault, Aaron," Liam said, hearing the sharp rise in his voice.

Aaron glared at Liam, then the map, seething.

"Given all of the information we have now, one thing becomes clear," Liam continued.

"The next operation that the scouts were talking about is probably another attack that Lemm wants to coordinate. Only question is where."

"It doesn't matter. The end result is the same." Aaron righted himself and glared at the string of exes that cluttered the map. "More dead imperials, and more Avats left to fend for themselves. Or to get thrown into a fiery pit." He thought back to the debriefing meeting from the day before.

His anger boiled. "Lemm lied to us. Right to our faces. He made it sound like the imperials found us by chance. But the whole time he was roping our scouts into a bloodbath, and we nearly took the fall for it. And if he's just been leaving the slaves behind during this…'revolution' of his, then he hasn't been doing any of this for their sake, either."

Liam said nothing.

Renée was equally quiet, her lips taut.

Aaron faced them. "If his next attack was supposed to be tonight then we still have time to find him and the scouts, and stop them. If we don't, Taranis and every slave in their path is in danger."

Liam nodded.

Renée took a deep breath. Calmed, she looked at Orion. "I'm surprised your brother told you all of this."

"He was trying to get me to sympathize with him," Orion said dismally. "He wanted me to join them. I tried to talk him out of it. The Empire's way too big for a village as small as us to try and take it down with brute force.

"I guess he got fed up with me," he sighed. "When I woke up he was gone." He frowned, remembering something. "Now that I think about it, he did say that the other scouts, and Lemm, were trying to recruit a lot more people from Taranis to join them."

Aaron's eyes narrowed with displeasure. After all its years of existence, the village was about to break off into factions now?

"He even said that one of them was gonna try to convince one of the more influential members of the village," Orion went on. He scratched his head. "It was gonna be either Aaron, Liam or Brent… but I can't remember."

Aaron stared at him.

Even Liam seemed disturbed, as did Renée.

Brent *had* been acting peculiar that day.

"Armor up." Aaron rounded on them both. His frown was

gone, but he looked no less urgent. "We're going after those scouts. I'll meet you both at Harver's so we can take her Skycrafts."

Liam and Renée nodded.

"Thanks, Orion. Clean this up." Aaron patted the map and rushed out of the room.

Liam and Renée took off after him.

"Hey!" Orion tried but they left too quickly. He faced the map helplessly, with his little exes made in charcoal. "How'm I supposed to clean this up…?"

Aaron didn't even feel like he touched the ground as he sprinted through Taranis. Darting between nighttime stragglers and barely apologizing to those he nearly knocked over, he made a beeline for his house and threw the door open.

When he got there, no one was home.

And Brent's room was empty.

71

HUNCHED AGAINST HIS saiga's spine Brent galloped across the valley, his eyes on the swelling foothills ahead of him. Tight-lipped and white-knuckled as he gripped his beast's yellow hair, he urged it to run faster.

After smuggling an imperial disguise from the Main House to his bedroom so he could change, he'd slinked his way through Taranis and towards the edge of the farmlands, where the saigas and horses were penned. The villager he'd spoken with had been confused by his desire for one of the swift yellow beasts, but he'd mitigated her fears by saying that the chief had ordered him to survey the edge of the valley for security reasons.

She'd believed him.

He'd noticed something strange at that point: the number of horses in the enclosure were less than normal.

"Oh," the villager had said when he'd pointed it out. "We woke up this morning and they were gone. While you're out, do you mind keeping an eye out for them? We're not sure how, but they might've escaped while we were asleep."

"I will," he promised.

Still now, he felt guilty for lying to her about Ivan's false order.

But it was too late to regret anything at this point. By now, Taranis had fallen so far behind him that no one would be able to tell who he was.

He wasn't doing any of this for his own sake, of course. Lemm had been right about Ivan, and even more right about what Taranis needed to do. Standing by, idle, while the Empire prepared to make its next move certainly wasn't the ideal option. Not now. Not while there were so many lives in the village that needed to be protected — lives that he had torn from the Empire's clutches himself.

He wasn't about to let them be ensnared again.

His jaw tight, he rode in the stillness of the dark for a moment longer, the foothills so near that he could dismount his beast and climb them on his own in a few minutes if he so wished. The barrier leading to Odelwhite wasn't too far now.

Suddenly, a gentle humming worked its way into his ears, bearing on him from above. It didn't sound like a normal wind, he deduced, and it didn't sound natural, either.

He pinched the skin at the base of his saiga's neck and with a low snort it pulled to a stop, its front hooves kicking the air. As soon as it planted them back in the grass, Brent twisted atop its back to see where the humming was coming from.

The Skycrafts were already descending towards him at that point, their undersides glowing from what he could only guess were the qazhë seeds that Harver had placed inside them. When they landed, he learned who was steering them.

Aaron appeared to him first, and as soon as his Skycraft touched the ground he hopped into the grass. He was dressed like an imperial, with a short cloak that was buttoned across his left shoulder and a belted jerkin, as well as thick leather boots that laced up along the calf.

Liam landed not far from him. He, too, had changed out of his village attire, swapping it for a tattered, high-collared poncho that covered him like a cloak and a close-fitted, seamed hat that hid the silhouette of his pointy ears. He also wore a pair of trousers that were tucked into buckled boots, and leather gauntlets with fingerless gloves were fitted to his arms.

Renée stepped out from behind him. Her black hair was tied into a loose ponytail that fell over her shoulder, and a bronze breastplate hugged her deep red tunic. Leather gauntlets covered her arms, and iron shin guards protected her sandaled legs.

"Thought it was you." Aaron looked anything but happy to see Brent. "Didn't think we'd catch you inside the valley."

Brent turned his saiga so that he could face them all completely. Aaron's words explained their manner of dress. "What're you guys doing out here?"

"I could ask you the same question." Aaron's eyes glinted fiercely. "But we've already figured that much out."

Brent said nothing.

"I'd like to do this the easy way." Aaron dropped a hand onto his tonfa in warning. "Turn back, Brent. You're crazy if you think that going with Lemm into the Empire is Taranis' last hope. If anything, it's the opposite."

Brent couldn't help but laugh. It was a small one and it lacked the true joy it usually carried. "What, you gonna knock me out if I refuse?"

"If we have to." Liam came forward. His sword was belted to the back of his waist.

Renée's expression was stiff but dour. Her sword was belted to her hip.

Brent's face dropped.

They were serious.

With his own expression falling into one of unfriendly resolve, he slid to the ground. "Even if that is what I'm doing, why's it such a problem?"

Aaron stared at him, the sides of his eyes constricting with careful observation. "You don't know what you're signing up for, do you?"

Brent met his stare with an unblinking one of his own.

"I thought you'd at least be smart enough to look into that on your own," Aaron scoffed. "You're being fooled. Lemm's hired you out to help him on his murder spree across the Empire."

Brent eyed him with a hard frown. "What?"

"Mekial told us something that he and his friends overheard while they were trapped in Odelwhite." Renée came forward. "The guardsmen attacked us because they thought they'd be able to arrest Saruke's Shade at the same time. Lemm."

Brent was disbelieving.

"He's been going across the Empire, killing any imperial he comes across. But that's not what bothers me." Aaron drew Brent's eyes to him. "For the past year he's been doing this, Brent. Killing slave owners and noblemen, only to leave their slaves to take the fall for it. Given how we don't have very many Liberation Fronts left standing, those slaves could've only faced one of two fates: either they were sold to new masters, or they were sacrificed to the imperial gods. We've got reason to believe that more cases are leaning towards the latter."

Brent didn't hide his shock.

"Then, our scouts joined him." Aaron's expression, by contrast, was tense. "That's why they hadn't been reporting in. It had nothing to do with fear of jeopardizing our location. Their string of assaults were so close to us that it got the Empire's attention, and led to their invasion. They already suspected Odelwhite as our hideout, but with all that extra activity they decided to move in. Lemm and the scouts may've helped us, but they were only trying to cover their own tracks.

"We found out that he's got another operation planned tonight," Aaron finished. "Whatever it is, and whatever he's talked you into, you're not gonna be helping Taranis. And you definitely won't be freeing any slaves."

Brent looked away again, his eyebrows drawing together.

Aaron eyed him impatiently, his lips pulled tight and his jaw tense. "Are you gonna say something?" he snapped.

Liam watched Brent stoically, waiting.

Renée looked uncertain, but stern.

When Brent looked at them, his face was unnaturally empty. "Back when I graduated," he started, "I wondered if auction raids were enough to change the Avats' situation. And I used to wonder...or hope, that it was. But after yesterday, I've realized that they're not."

Aaron wasn't keen on losing the argument. "You do realize that the only reason yesterday happened was because your long-last friend is a psychopath? You think more of what he's doing is the answer?"

"Not quite. But we can't just stand down either, waiting to see what the Empire will do next. So if Pops won't make a move, I'll add my strength to someone who will. You might as well tag along." Brent nodded at their outfits. "You're ready for it. I'm on my way to see Lemm right now, and find out what his plan is."

"Even after what we just told you?" Renée was stunned.

Brent looked at her. His brow was tight. "Yes."

She stared at him.

He snorted. "C'mon, you guys know who I am. I've always got a trick up my sleeve. D'you really think I'm just gonna join Lemm and kill people mindlessly? I care about the slaves." His face was grim. "All of them. No matter what it looks like, I'm not gonna leave them to figure things out on their own. But I can't stay here, twiddling my thumbs, either."

Aaron glared at him, still cautious, and his hand fell towards the handle of his tonfa.

Brent's gaze darted from that small motion to Aaron's face. His own expression hardened. "I'm just taking your advice, Aaron. It's time for us to show the imperials who they're messing with. For the sake of every slave, and every one of us that they've ever taken."

Aaron's face stiffened and his hand froze. His mind whirred for a minute, recognizing the words that he himself had said, and for a second he seemed to be on the verge of relenting.

But then, flexing his fingers, he unholstered both of his tonfa and stepped forward.

"Not this time." Twirling them against his forearms, he held them up in preparation of a fight. "And it's not because I doubt your ambition. It's because this whole thing smells foul. Someone who can kill and lie as easily as Lemm does, and then just abandons the people that he claims to be doing it for, is no friend of ours. And I doubt any of this'll go your way at all.

"I'll only say it one more time: turn back." He smiled dangerously. "Or I'll just knock you out like in our training days and drag you back."

"Don't think I'm standing by." Liam stepped forward and reached for the hilt of his sword. His normally blank face had hardened into a scowl. "I'm with Aaron on this one, Brent. You're in over your head."

Brent looked at Renée.

Her face showed conflict and reluctance. And in his, she saw a gentle yearning as he searched for her understanding.

Her heart wavered and her palms grew sweaty.

Finally, she set her face against him.

"Brent," her voice was solemn, "you know we don't want to fight you over this. Please — stand down."

He closed his eyes and emitted a disappointed sigh.

Then with a battle-ready look, he drew his bladed staffs, locked them together, and spun his weapon into a proper grip. "You first."

At that even the wind became silent, shocked by his steadfast resolve.

A second later Aaron shifted, dug a foot into the ground. Kicking off of it, he shot towards Brent like an arrow.

Brent braced himself, readied his staff.

Aaron didn't hold any punches: tonfa whirling he tore at Brent's defenses, striking, kicking, seeking to twist around his staff so he could close in and get a clean hit at Brent's head.

But Brent was grounded, rooted in his stances, and with a pointed gaze he matched Aaron blow for blow, countering his aggression with an equally matched strength. Every time their weapons collided the heavy cry of metal made the air shudder; it ignited their senses, magnified their focus. Though knowing one another's moves almost as well as they knew their own they remained ever-vigilant, leaning not on casual familiarity but the heavy reality that this was no sparring match. It was a disagreement, however small or large either of them viewed it.

So the stakes were different. Higher.

For losing here wouldn't end with just a bruised ego.

Parrying Aaron, Brent swung his staff at an upward angle, meaning to take him off his feet.

But Aaron leaped out of the way and Liam took his place.

With an assault that was like a destructive dance, the Northern Avat assailed Brent without pause, not even a break in his gaze.

At long last he, too, was forced back, raising his sword in defense when Brent swung his staff at him so hard that the air vibrated.

Absorbing the blow and using it as momentum, Liam retreated several feet in a single bound.

Renée closed in next, jumping out of his shadow to catch Brent by surprise.

But he'd already heard her.

Just before her sword could arc in to disarm him, he split his weapon in half and caught the edge of her blade against both of his own.

The two traded blows for a moment, shredding the night sky with the clanging of swords and the thumping of feet —

Then she pirouetted out of his reach and back-flipped to get some distance.

Golden eyes cold, Brent cut his bladed staffs across the air and rushed in again, seeking another round.

⚔

Harver made one final adjustment to the handlebar of the Skycraft that she was working on. To secure the change, she twisted the retractable pole until it clicked.

"Finally…" she breathed and with one arm she wiped the sweat away from beneath her bangs. Her pointy ears tingled abruptly.

She twisted to face the road and got to her feet when she recognized the footsteps that were approaching. She didn't need to see the person's face to be sure of who it was. "Hey, Eklaire!"

Hardly a second later, Eklaire herself came around the bend. She stopped when she saw what Harver had been tinkering on in her yard.

This Skycraft's deck was smaller than the ones that she'd unveiled the day before, and it could probably only hold two riders at once. The rubbershroom material that lined its edges was also much thicker, though its smooth texture still offered the board that same aerodynamic shape. As for its handle, which was retractable, it didn't reach all the way to the deck. Rather, it stopped halfway there.

The propellers were also different: there was a weighted bottom on this one, giving the craft the equivalent of a beer belly with a flat base. There was only one large vent on the bottom, which was closed, and at its rear there was one set of open propellers. Meanwhile, at the front, the Skycraft had something that was akin to a bottled nose.

"Uh…" Eklaire made a strange face. "Whatcha got there, Harver?"

"I'm fixing up an older model of the Skycrafts," the inventor answered. "I had Brent swing by earlier to let me know how the other ones worked out for him yesterday, and I've been using his suggestions to upgrade this old clunker."

Eklaire frowned at it. "Looks old."

"To be honest, I started making it a couple of years ago, but it kept breaking down on me," Harver confessed. "Finally, I made the models that you guys saw yesterday, thinking that streamlining their look would make it easier for them to fly. But even those were hard to finalize. Tyre's actually the one who helped me out."

Intrigued, Eklaire eyed her playfully. "Really? Tyre, huh?"

Harver huffed indignantly. "He started touching stuff without my permission. It just sorta happened."

"Mhm."

Harver saw the look on her face and promptly rolled her eyes. Eklaire giggled.

"Anyway, after plugging some qazhë seeds into it I've been playing around with it every now and again." Harver kicked the clunky Skycraft. "But it still needs more work."

"Yeah." Eklaire wrinkled her nose and looked the vehicle over. "It definitely don't look as good as the other ones."

"Yeah, I know…anyway, what're you doing here?"

"I was lookin' fer Ren actually! But I can't find her nowhere. So I tried lookin' for Brent but then I couldn't find him nowhere, neither. Then I tried lookin' for Liam, but that didn't work out."

"Huh…Aaron, Ren and Liam offered to help me test out the other Skycrafts, actually." Harver returned to the ground and fished through her satchel for something. "I'd finished making a few repairs on them and they said they'd go ahead and take 'em for a spin.

PEDAL TO THE METAL
CODE: WEIRDLIGHT

They seemed to be in a hurry, though…I don't know where Brent is."

"Oh." Eklaire paused with a potent frown. "Wait, that don't seem weird to you?"

Harver pinched her finger with one of her tools and yelped. "Well —"

A soundless blast of light erupted in the farthest reaches of the valley, igniting like the sun.

Harver whipped around to see it, shading her eyes at the same time.

Eklaire did similar.

When the glow died at last, Harver lowered her hand with a look of bewilderment. "What in the world was that? A flash orb?"

"Think so," Eklaire said, blinking furiously to clear up her vision.

Harver's frown became inquisitive. "Let's check it out." She hopped aboard the Skycraft and, after adjusting the handle, turned it on. "C'mon!"

"What?!" Eklaire backed away from the floating board. "No way, uh-uh! This girl's better off on the ground! That's why I like bein' barefoot, cuz I love feelin' solid ground between my toes so much!"

"Don't be such a potato, c'mon!" Snatching her by the elbow, Harver hauled her aboard.

Eklaire clung to her like a terrified cat.

"Don't squeeze me so tight, I'm tiny," Harver said absently, testing the handlebar's rotation.

"Harver…" Eklaire whimpered and with her knees buckling, she tried to find some form of balance. "You are crazier than a rund-over dog…"

"That's how I make cool stuff!" Rolling the handlebar's button, Harver pushed it.

A gale gunned out of the Skycraft's vent, making the whole thing wobble, and it rocketed into the sky and over the village.

Eklaire's screaming trailed into the distance.^{tv}

Sitting atop a small boulder near the valley barrier, Lemm tilted his terrible mask in his hand to study it in the moonlight. His eyes flicked up when he heard the clamor of approaching hoofbeats.

In time a saiga appeared over the rise of the hill and galloped towards him. Recognizing its rider, he got to his feet with a smile.

"Well, well. Look who it is." Lemm watched Brent hop to the ground when he was close. "I'm guessing you're responsible for that big flash of light I just saw. Ran into some trouble?"

Brent glanced over his shoulder. "Yeah. Little bit."

"And you shook 'em off, looks like." Lemm clearly approved. "So, you're here. That means the chief issued a stand-down order."

Brent held his knowing gaze firmly. "Yeah."

Lemm smirked. "Predictable." He beckoned someone out of the shadows.

The Avat woman who appeared wasn't someone that Brent knew. She was tall and brown-skinned with razored black hair, and her clothes were plain and weathered.

"Izma, if you would." Lemm gestured to the barrier.

Casting Brent a disdainful look, the woman turned to the barrier and stretched her hands to it.

Brent started when her quintessence touched the air, mingling with the aether. In the next second, the barrier actually leaned to obey her will.

"Surprised?" Lemm looked at him, entertained. "Izma's what you'd call an outlier. An Avat aetheriest. Who'da thunk they even existed?"

Brent only stared at her in bewilderment.

"Like a lot of people you're about to meet, she's a runaway." Lemm watched the barrier creak and shift alongside him. "She's innate, apparently. As soon as her master found out, like any Arkanian slave master woulda done, he tried to have her killed. But, she actually managed to escape. Then, I found her." His smile changed, deepening with malevolence. "She's got a lot of potential. But boy has she got a temper."

The trees and vines stopped moving. The barrier was open. Izma looked at them.

"You're in for a lot more surprises." Lemm started into the forest.

"Not so fast," Brent interrupted.

Lemm turned.

"You still haven't told me what your alternative is." Brent was flat-footed. "After I hear it, I'll decide whether or not I want to go with you. I heard about what you've really been up to over the past year," he added quietly. "Don't count me in as some brainless follower."

Lemm smiled, but it was thin and heartless. "Right, of course. You're Skylok, after all."

Brent waited.

Lemm didn't make him wait long. "We're gonna raid Lyrik Estate."

72

"H ANG ON!" HARVER shouted. Shoving the handle forward, she dove for the valley.

Eklaire's head flew back from the force, her white hair flying. She nearly got whiplash when Harver ripped the handle back, leveling them over the earth. Grass and wildflowers flipped into the sky as they roared over them.

When three people appeared in her vision, Harver released the accelerator.

The Skycraft didn't stop.

Aaron, Renée and Liam, still disoriented from the blinding flash orb that had gone off in the middle of their fight, heard the incoming craft.

Fortunately they didn't have to dodge it, for Harver twisted the Skycraft away, hoping she could make it skid to a halt.

It worked, and she and Eklaire slid to a shaky stop in front of a lonely tree. A shallow trench marked their route.

Aaron stood, blinking through the lights that still popped in the corners of his eyes. It took him a second to recognize them. "What the…?"

Liam faced them quietly, still waiting for his vision to return with a troubled frown.

"Harver?" Renée stepped towards them, squinting. "Eklaire? What're you doing out here?"

Harver disembarked the Skycraft with wobbly knees and an

even wobblier voice. "Man…I don't think I've flown that one in too long…it's a bit finicky…"

"We're alive!" Eklaire stumbled into the grass and fell to her hands and knees, her head bowed. "I can't believe we're alive!"

Harver was the first to notice their friends and she pieced together a story at the sight of their disoriented looks. She smiled tauntingly. "What happened? You guys have some trouble with your Skycrafts, too?"

"No." Aaron slipped his tonfa back into their holsters. "They work fine."

Liam put his sword back into its sheath.

Renée went to Eklaire and helped her up.

"Ooh…" she groaned woozily, holding her head. She frowned at Renée's disheveled look. "What happened to ya'll? You look like you got put through the ringer! What is this, some kinda late-night sparrin' session?"

"It's a long story," Aaron sighed, his eyes falling.

"Well, it ain't like we don't got time," Eklaire pointed out, now balanced enough to stand on her own.

Aaron traded looks with Renée and Liam, who looked both sad and pensive respectively.

"You know the fires from yesterday?" Renée asked, turning to look at Eklaire.

"Yeah?"

"Well, those weren't just imperials who were invading. It was Empyrean's Guard."

Eklaire clearly didn't like the sound of that. Nor did Harver.

"That's how the scouts came back. They'd allied themselves with someone named Lemm from the Empire, and helped us get rid of the guardsmen. He used to be a friend of Taranis. But…it doesn't seem that way anymore."

"What do you mean by that?" Harver asked cautiously.

"I'll explain," Liam said and he did just that, telling the girls of how the scouts who'd returned had left the village again last night, prompting the three of them to hunt fruitlessly for Lemm, since their absence was tied to him. He went on to tell them about Orion and the knowledge that he'd shared, and concluded with how Brent had decided to join Lemm's bloodthirsty cause.

"What?!" Eklaire exclaimed.

"Why would he do that?" Harver actually sounded like she was hoping for a legitimate answer. "If he does, won't he just be putting slaves in more danger?"

"Don't know what he's thinking. We tried to stop him."

"Yeah. Then he threw a flash orb and ran off." Aaron rubbed his eyes irritably. "He's gonna pay for that."

Renée looked away, crestfallen.

"But I don't know." Aaron was quiet for a while. "Maybe I can see why he's doing it."

"What do you mean?" Liam asked.

"The Liberation Fronts have only been around for a bit longer than I have," Aaron started. "But we hadn't made any kind of headway in rescuing slaves until Brent graduated last year. Until then, we kept losing as many people as we saved. And that goes for every one of our sister villages. Despite everything that we did, the slave trade kept running. Our raids barely nicked it. And no matter how many slaves we rescued, there always seemed to be more for the Empire to shop around.

"I hate what I see out there, every time I go." His eyes became unfocused. "Avats crouching in dark corners for fear of their lives with their bones showing; slave traders shoving them around like worthless objects at auctions; children being torn from their mothers and no one even batting an eye; and slaves that pissed off the wrong master are struck dead in broad daylight. Their masters get fined for it, but what's that compared to the loss of a life?" He looked up drearily, his sight going past the stars to stare into an eternal void that could offer him no answer. "It's enough to make anyone with a conscience go insane. In that case, maybe we aren't being bold enough."

"Bold enough?" Renée echoed. Circling to see him head-on, she glared at him. "You're an auction raider, Aaron. Not to mention you sneak off on your own all the time to do your own assignments, to do more than what you're asked. How is that not bold enough?"

"Because we're still exactly where we started." He was hardly fazed by her confrontation.

She thought to retort. But nothing came to mind for her to say.

"So you're just gonna let Brent run off with a crazy murderer?!" Eklaire flung her hands into the air. "I may not get what ya'll have to deal with when ya head on out to the Empire, but if I know anythin', y'can't let Brent go off'n do what he's about to do! It ain't even what Taranis does!"

"He did say he would keep the slaves in mind," Liam reminded Aaron. "As sudden as his departure was, I don't think he's capable of letting them down the way that Lemm and the scouts have."

Aaron considered that.

"I'm going after him."

The two looked at Renée, whose resolute face spoke volumes. "Maybe he thinks this is his last option. But there has to be a better way. One that doesn't involve him being around someone as dangerous as Lemm. It's like you said, Aaron," she looked at him, "someone who can kill and lie as easily as he does is no friend of ours. I don't trust him."

Aaron was quiet. But he bowed his chin in agreement.

"What about you? Or do you just not care anymore?"

"That's not true." Aaron stared off towards the ends of the valley. "Brent was raised with me, remember? He's my brother."

Renée's severe expression softened a bit.

"My really *stupid* brother," Aaron added, his eyebrow twitching angrily. He sighed. "I'm going, too. I don't care what his reasons are." He faced Renée. "He's gonna get even more Avats killed. And I'm not gonna let that happen."

"You don't know which way they're going," Liam told them. "How will you find him?"

"A Skycraft," Aaron said decidedly.

Harver scoffed. "Hey! Those're *my* Skycrafts you're talking about. You can't just take them on a sky-trip without going through me first!"

"It's important." He faced her. His hard face had eased, and his eyes were soft with earnesty. "Please."

Harver tried frowning at him with her arms folded. At long last she gave in with a heavy groan and a roll of her eyes. Color even bloomed in her cheeks. "Fine. But if you break them," she pointed at him with her eyes narrowed, "I'm breaking *you.*"

He smiled.

She blushed. Crossing her arms again, she turned away.

"And you Liam?" Aaron faced him.

The Northern Avat looked between them all for a second, thoughtful. "I'll come. You might need ears like mine."

"And patience," Renée added, sliding Aaron a knowing look.

He frowned at her.

"Eklaire." Liam looked at her. "Tell Lilian that I'm keeping my promise."

She saluted. "You got it!"

He smiled gently.

"Whoa!" Her green and blue eyes grew. "Hey, y'know, smiles really suit you, Liam!"

He turned away sharply. But everyone could see the pink in his cheeks.

"Well, we'd better get going." Aaron headed over to the Skycraft he'd flown in on. "We don't wanna give Brent too much of a head start."

Renée climbed aboard the other, and Liam stepped on behind her.

"Remember how to fly it?" he asked.

"Think so…" She started adjusting the handle and fixing her foot into the strap.

"Be careful, okay?" Harver said, approaching Aaron.

He looked up at her and nodded with a crooked smile. "Thanks."

She smiled back.

Placing a hand on Harver's back, Eklaire gave the raiders a bracing smile of her own. "Ya'll come back now, y'hear?"

"Right." There was a small change in Aaron's gaze when he looked at her, a gentleness that hadn't been there previously.

It was only present for a second. Eklaire hadn't noticed it, but Harver did question it. For some reason, it made her stomach clench.

Aaron turned his board on. "Okay. Here we go!"

His Skycraft hummed and levitated, wind blowing out from

under it. Pressing the accelerator, he soared into the sky.

Renée and Liam took off after him, leaving Harver and Eklaire to watch them disappear into the twinkling night sky.

⁂

Odelwhite looked as green as it ever did when Brent stepped through the barrier. But a simple turn of the head allowed him to see the scarred trees and ash-gray earth that lay to the south, leading to where most of the destruction was contained.

Lemm and Izma walked him in the other direction, to the north. It wasn't long before they came to a clearing, where an arm of the river trickled through softly.

Noticing that they weren't alone, Brent stopped.

Vagabonds littered the area, totaling to just about thirteen people. They were an eclectic mix, ranging from mercenaries to runaways, and unlike Izma they were all Arkanians. All sorts of weapons were strapped to their backs or belted to their sides, and only a few were conversing at a dull murmur.

But when they saw that their leader had returned, they shifted their attention.

"That's him?" a woman asked, looking at Brent. She was sharpening her axe by the river. "Skylok. Huh."

Brent said nothing to her.

She smiled. "Way more handsome than I thought he'd be."

Brent looked out at everyone else.

"No need to be uncomfortable." Lemm joined the gathering along with Izma. "I already told them about you."

"Thanks." Brent only passed another slow look over the crowd. "Where're the scouts?"

"Gone ahead. But we'll outpace them soon enough."

The woman who'd been sharpening her axe stood up. "I'd ask what the poster-child for Avat liberation wants with us," she began, moving to stand next to Lemm, "but I guess it doesn't matter. We've all got our own reasons for hating the Empire."

Brent turned his eyes from her to the darkness of the clearing. His ears twitched when something cracked in the distance.

Something was watching them.

Lifting his chin, Lemm whistled crisply.

The trees whispered back and the shadows danced. Everywhere Lemm's followers stood up and prepared themselves, as if his sound was a signal to depart.

But they didn't go anywhere.

Brent eyed them all carefully, suspiciously.

A moment later, a group of high-backed creatures crept out of the trees with bared teeth and moonlit claws.

He sucked in a breath.

They were crocuta.

Hunchbacked beasts with spotted coats, they had powerful jaws that were armed with fangs as sharp as any sword. They snarled into the clearing, ears up and thick manes of black hair stretching along their arching spines. Some were almost as tall as a mounted horseman, while others were slightly shorter. But all stalked forth with shoulders that spanned at least a meter across and legs that were as thick as tree trunks.

As far as Brent knew, crocuta were deadly, nocturnal fiends that weren't native to Lyrik. No, they belonged to the wastelands that ran alongside the great gorge in Lenora, which split the province in half; there, they made their homes in sinister caves, barren terrain and mountainous badlands. They served no master aside from their abysmal stomachs and sought no prey aside from that which wandered into their territory.

But each of these crocuta were wearing two large saddles atop their mighty backs.

Brent's eyes snapped to Lemm, who didn't even move as one of the crocuta neared him. When it was close, he patted its snout.

Brent's face twitched in a flicker of horror and amazement. Had Lemm actually tamed these creatures?

Wordlessly, he watched as Lemm and the rest of his accomplices climbed into the carnivores' saddles.

"There's a free seat." Lemm jabbed his thumb behind him. "You can ride with me."

Setting his jaw, Brent dropped his eyes to his crocuta.

It was larger than the others. If this group had been a wild clan, it likely would've been the leader.

Its black eyes hung inches above Brent's own and it twisted towards him deliberately, its thick lips curled to flaunt grinding fangs. Lifting an ebony paw it came closer, bringing its wet nose nearer to his face, and he took a careful step backward.

It glared at him, pupils dilated to fill its eyes with a black so deep that it was like peering into the maw of a chasm. Moonlight caught its fur, glistening across the ends of its straight-haired coat and lining every fearsome wrinkle in its sneering face.

At its back, its kin watched it closely. They almost seemed eager to see how it would react to the newcomer.

Brent retreated again, just as slowly.

He broke a twig.

The crocuta's sneering jaw popped open with a roar that struck him with the stench of feces and rotten flesh. Teeth flashing, it lunged for his head.

Hissing, Lemm jerked on the reins that were hooked into the sides of its mouth. Small blades lined the bit that it was attached to and so with Lemm's tug they pierced the beast's flesh, causing it to tear its face away from Brent with a devastating howl.

Brent's skin crawled.

The other crocuta flinched. Some flipped their ears back and crouched a little.

Blood as black as ink leaked over the lips of their leader and it snarled fiercely, derisively. At last it huffed and with its face turned to the trees, it showed no further interest in Brent.

Brent on the other hand, continued to stare at it, a bead of sweat gliding down his nape. His heart was still pounding.

"Funny, she's not usually so uptight." Lemm's eyes twinkled with malicious jest. "Maybe she's hungry."

His crocuta snarled venomously.

Lemm reached into one of the packs that was strapped near him and produced from it a large slab of raw meat. He tossed it over the crocuta's head.

Smelling the treat, the beast snapped it up.

"Climb on." Lemm's eyes were on Brent now. "We've got a lot of ground to cover."

Passing the crocuta one last glance as it finished its meal, Brent approached its hide and climbed into its second seat.

"Axelius is three days away on horseback, if you account for breaks." Lemm looked over his troupe. "On crocuta, it'll take us about a day less. Remember, we travel by night. And we rendezvous outside the city wall. Meet up by the southern entrance, on the hilltop."

His followers nodded mutely.

"See you on the other side," Lemm said, his voice chilling, and he kicked his beast's sides.

Brent felt its muscles bulge beneath him and in the next instant they were zooming forward, racing through the trees so quickly that everything around him looked like a blur. It was as if he was riding atop the land-version of a Skycraft. Not even saigas were known to run this fast.

He heard everyone else depart the same way, heard the rush of wind as crocutas snarled past him to take differing routes to their destination.

He clutched the saddle.

This was it, then.

There was no turning back now.

✒︎

Elder Qaçai had been furious when he'd learned what Oruviçu had done in Odelwhite Forest. With his features sharpening, his already glowing eyes had gained an even brighter shine before he'd rebuked his subordinate. His rage could've matched the eruption of a long-dormant volcano.

Oruviçu hadn't objected to any of it. He'd simply accepted the reprimands in willful silence with his eyes downcast.

When he'd finally taken a break from his shouting, the elder had let loose a drained sigh. "But...I can understand why you did it, at least," he relented. "And I suppose I should be thanking you. My grandson would probably be dead if you hadn't stepped in."

Oruviçu hadn't answered.

And he hadn't stayed either. In fact ever since his meeting with the elder had ended, he'd been here —

At the ruins of Çaru'qu's Temple.

Tucked behind the southern reaches of the Adriak Mountains, the temple was in complete shambles. Shattered columns and crumbling capitals littered the cracked and desolate earth, and dead trees stood where beautiful gardens had once been. Thorny vines grew out of the ground to trap broken staircases, and the reliefs that had been carved into the walls and portico were wearing away.

An echo of the temple's former glory could be seen in its general structure. It had been a peripteral building, surrounded by porticos and columns, and had been completely enclosed by a colonnade. Its pillars, now half their size, had been built to reach for the stars, whose glimmering bodies now peeked through a thickening coat of storm clouds.

Somewhere far off, Oruviçu could hear thunder rolling through those clouds, and every so often lightning would flash in tandem. With every glint of light a different part of the temple's fading reliefs would be unveiled: a crowd here; a ceremony there; a webbed wing; dancing flames…but with the isolated images being scattered across the temple walls, there was no way for them to form any sort of cohesive narrative.

Not that Oruviçu needed one.

After all…he knew the story.

CRRACK!!!
BA-BOOOM...

YOU'VE ALWAYS WORKED ON THE FRINGES OF OUR REALITY.
NOW, MILLENNIA LATER, YOU'VE ALL BUT BEEN ERASED FROM OUR HISTORY...
...SCARCELY REMEMBERED, IF EVER EVEN ACKNOWLEDGED.
YET YOU STILL CALL TO US.
FAINTLY.

I SUPPOSE...
SHFF...
...WE CAN NO LONGER AVOID THE INEVITABLE.

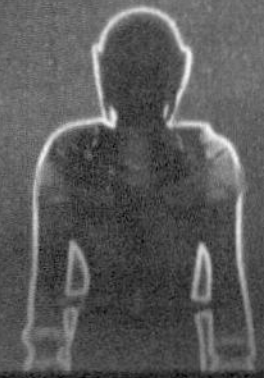

MAY THE BLOOD THAT THAT BOY CARRIES...
...UNDO THIS ALL.
SO THAT THE BLOOD THAT YOU SHED...
...WON'T HAVE BEEN IN VAIN...

...ZION.
FWOOOO...
CRRAASH!!
BA-BOOOM!

THE AVAT PRINCE WILL CONTINUE IN VOL. 9...

The Avat Prince will continue in Volume 9...

URLING UP BENEATH *his blankets, Brent buried his face into his pillow. The night was quiet all around him in his royal bedchambers…until a strange whisper pervaded the empty space.*

"You…"

He curled up tighter, his eyebrows furrowing.

"You…"

He opened his eyes, frowning through the gloom until his vision came into focus.

Someone was standing at his bedside.

With the painted walls of his boyhood room as a backdrop, a young Emperor Koberius loomed beside him. His left eye was disfigured, slitted. The red mark inside of it was glowing mightily.

Young Brent's heart lurched into his throat.

Koberius' eyes were wide. "You tainted my bloodline, didn't you?"

Brent awoke with a start, his breathing sharp and heavy. When he'd calmed, he twisted onto his side and got to his feet.

He, Lemm, Lemm's followers and the scouts were all camped on a hill that overlooked Axelius. Shaking off his nightmare, he wandered to the edge of the hill and looked out over the city.

Lemm had been right about it only taking two nights to arrive. The following day, Kyrah, Aizen, and the other scouts of Taranis had joined them.

Now, night had again covered the earth in a darkness sprinkled with stars.

Now, they moved.

Lifting his eyes from the Commoners' District, he looked over the gleaming band of black that was the Atteline River. From there, he set his sights on the magnificent structures that festooned the Nobility District.

Towering pediments crowded its rooftops, laced pilasters decorated the doorposts, sensual marble statues hovered over sparkling fountains, imperial banners billowed in the wind, torchlight speckled the roads and winked through windows…

Nostalgia couldn't even pinch him.

He had envied every person that had lived in that district for living the life that he was supposed to have. He still remembered the bite of hunger that had gnawed on him on most nights, along with the terror of being enslaved, and the fear that he'd never find anyone to turn to or hide with…

He dropped his gaze.

A sea of colorful trees rolled away from the hill, separating him from the stone wall that wrapped around Axelius. If he looked keenly enough, he could see that soldiers were patrolling the parapets. The nearest portcullis had also been lowered.

Something rustled behind him.

He turned.

A man in a mask was standing on the opposite side of the camp, stiff and silent before the trees.

Brent froze.

It wasn't Lemm, he determined, for a quick look revealed that Lemm was still asleep near the campfire's remains, as were the other members of their traveling party. However, the masks that he and this stranger owned were perfectly identical, from the shape of the mane to the mark of the Liberation Fronts that was painted across its forehead.

Brent squinted confusedly. "Who —?"

The man walked away before he could finish.

Even as he did, Brent glimpsed the image of someone else appear over him, like a ghost: someone with sky-blue hair that trailed towards his ankles, and narrow eyes that carried the light of the galaxies.

Without a word, he vanished into the trees.

Hardly thinking, Brent tore after him.

"Wait!" he cried, and he stumbled into a moonlit glade.

The masked man was already there, clearly waiting for him.

Brent chanced a few careful steps closer. "That mask," he started. "Didn't know somebody else had it."

The stranger offered no response.

"Was it you, then?" Brent pressed. "The one who showed up in Taranis, during our celebration. Even —"

Wind bustled through the branches and shivered through the leaves.

He squinted against it and once more he glimpsed that same shadow, that ghost of a blue-haired man hovering in front of the Shade —

Another gale came and he cast his arms in front of his eyes —

And then everything stopped.

When he lowered his arms, the nightly world had been traded for shifting clouds of teal, and gold, and specks of white that drifted like diamonds cast into the sun.

Recognizing it all he twisted, then spun around to see this world and all of its gentle colors.

It was different this time: less than a figment of his imagination, and more than tangible. The air hummed quietly, as if in song, and although this realm was filled with empty space it didn't feel isolating. Not even lonely. It was as if the very air carried the presence of something that was infinitely greater than himself: something near, and warm.

Circling one last time, he faced the Shade once more.

To his shock, the man with blue hair was standing in his place. The clouds and light drifted in front of him, hiding his face, but his lean form and ornamented clothing were still in full view.

Suddenly the man spoke, and his voice echoed as if he was standing in the heart of some vaulted chamber:

"So, you've returned." Although Brent couldn't see his eyes, he knew in his gut that the man was looking right at him. *"After all this time…to right the wrongs of your past."*

Brent blinked at him, staring.

"That's why you really agreed to come, isn't it?" the stranger went on, still covered in that shifting light. *"Returning to Lyrik Estate would hold no other meaning to you than that."*

Brent tensed, his hackles rising.

How did this man know what he was doing?

"Who are you? Really." He steadied himself, his jaw set. "I've told other people about this place, y'know. And about you." He paused. "Some of them even think that you might be Zion himself. But," he shook his head, "that can't be right."

"Oh? You disagree with them?" Was it his imagination, or was the man smiling? *"And who do you think I am?"*

"I don't…" The sides of Brent's eyes flinched and a thought occurred to him — or rather, a memory: a time of being trapped in the lower chambers of a manor, of being caught by a boy with an unholy stare, of being strangled —

A flash of white light, and the glimpse of a man with gleaming eyes and trailing, sky-blue hair —

Brent grunted and he touched his forehead. The memories faded. "No, wait…you were…" He looked up, his narrow eyes tight with disbelief. "You were there…"

This time, he was sure that the man smiled. *"We have a lot of catching up to do,"* he said, *"and little time to do it. The aether"* — he looked up at the humming world around them — *"is strained. Soon, it will break…but truthfully, that was inevitable from the beginning."*

"Break?" Brent stepped forward. "What are you talking about?"

"Do you desire answers?" The man's attention fell to him once more. *"If you seek them, you'll find them. But only if you're seeking them in the right place."*

"What's that supposed to mean?" Brent hardly noticed that this heavenly realm was starting to retract, pulling all of its clouds and light inward.

"'Why won't the suffering of the Avat people come to an end? Why does the Empire desire their blood as sacrifice? Will it ever be possible to save them all?' And also," the man's invisible gaze seemed to rip into Brent's core, *"why was the boy with the demon's eye so bent on killing you? 'Spawn of Zion.'"*

Brent started. "That's —!"

"*You can only find so many answers in Axelius,*" the man went on and the receding winds gathered around him, tossing his hair and cloak about. "*Still, you had to go back. But if you find that you're still dissatisfied, then go to the ruins of Çaru'qu's Temple. There, you'll find the answers that you're looking for.*"

"Çaru'qu?" Brent stepped forward again, stunned. "You know who that is?!"

He grunted, his arms flying up when the retreating winds increased. It was like standing in a cyclone that was howling in reverse.

"Where am I even supposed to find it?!" he shouted.

"*Go to the Western Lowlands. There, I will meet you again myself.*"

Brent dared to squint through his arms.

The world was full of light. But even through its blinding glare, the blue-haired man was in his line of sight.

"*There's a lot to tell you, Brent. And not all the answers that you find will be the ones that you want.*"

It was difficult for Brent to tell whether or not the man was speaking out loud, or talking directly into his head now.

"*But even then —*"

The man smiled, and Brent saw his face for the first time: the galactic glow in his eyes faded, revealing a set of narrow, golden irises that matched the raider's own, and his pointed ears framed his angular face. He was young, having aged into the prime of his life, and there was a certain kindness about him that permeated the atmosphere.

"*— Çaru'qu doesn't make mistakes.*"

"Wait!" Brent shot up, breathless.

He was back at camp.

Getting to his feet, he checked the area perplexedly, expecting to see the blue-haired stranger and that world of light all over again again.

He didn't.

He frowned fuzzily. Had it been a dream?

"Look who's finally awake."

Brent swung around.

Lemm and the others were standing at the edge of the hill, facing Axelius.

As for Lemm he was looking at Brent, mask in hand.

Brent stared at it for a moment, gathering his wits as he determined what was reality and what wasn't.

Quietly, he picked up his staff and joined the group.

Lemm watched him. "Ready?"

Brent turned from him to Axelius. It was a moment before he replied.

When he did, any uncertainty that had been tickling his mind broke away. Determination settled in its place. "As I'll ever be."

Right, he thought, steeling himself for a future that looked as uncertain as it ever did.

There's no going back now.

⟢ ✄ ⟣

"Weh-heh-hell, now! Look who we have here…" Tossing an Arkanian prune up and down in his hand, Zarë'qu followed the edge of one of the cliffs that ringed the Peaks of Dover. His eyes, shaded by the black eyeholes of his mask, were fixed on a solitary figure that awaited him just ahead. "Viorë'to, The Dancing Blade of Aion…here in the flesh."

Hearing him, Viorë'to turned from the horizon. With the angle of her frame, she could see him just over her shoulder.

Thanks to the elevation of the Peaks of Dover, which were fixed at the southernmost reaches of Lenora Province, the ocean was fully visible beyond the continental shore. The great watery expanse existed as a flat sheet of glass along the horizon, and above it hung arcing clouds that glistened against the pink-and-purple sky. The last of the sun's light was gleaming beneath it all, striking the very edge of the world with a glow that resembled the rarest of gemstones.

The fading light cast long shadows across the clifftop, and it gleamed around the silhouettes of the two foreigners as they came together, on this precipice at the end of everything.

"Rare to see you on my turf." Zarë'qu bit into the prune as he closed the gap between them. "Might I suggest looking north? The Southern Mines really sparkle around this time of day, what with all those giant crystals poking out of it."

Taking his own advice, he snatched another bite out of the fruit and looked towards the sky-scraping mines. Sure enough, the crystal pillars and gemstone towers that sprouted out of the mountains were glowing softly, gracing the laborious work site with an other-worldly light.

He took another bite out of the prune and his eyes panned across the scene, from the rocky Southern Mines to the magnificent chasm that cut into the earth beside it. Only part of it was visible, of course, with the rest of it vanishing into the swirling desert sands as it stretched across the Empire.

Known as Zenrikk's Gorge, the great divide spanned almost the entire length of Lenora Province, splitting it right down the middle. Thanks to the light that fell from the crystal columns, its jagged crevices and sprawling cracks were softly illuminated, as was the visible stretch of desert wasteland that enclosed it.

Even from where Zarë'qu stood it was a terrifying thing to behold, with walls that were swathed in shadow and an earthen floor that couldn't be seen from above. There were tales that no one had ever traveled into its depths and returned, and Zarë'qu himself doubted that there was a bottom to it at all. The whole thing probably stretched deep into the earth, breaking through layers of bedrock to reach the planet's beating heart somewhere far below. The crocuta who nested in its caves didn't even descend after a certain point, as fearsome as they were. If that didn't speak to the dangers of the gorge, Zarë'qu wasn't sure what did.

"Hm…yep." He nodded to himself, retreating from his momentarily dark reverie. "Nothing like gazing into the depths of the earth at the end of the day! Doesn't give me the creeps at all. Hey, Vi" — he turned to Viorë'to and called to her from where he was — "what say we switch regions, huh? This little slice of Lenora and

Dukaris, for your little piece of Nassaul and Sylvonis. What do you say? The elder doesn't have to know!"

Viorë'to met his gaze as he spoke to her, but at the utterance of his question she dropped her head, seeming unsure. If anything, however, it was clear that her uncertainty wasn't connected to the implication of his rhetorical request.

The only sign of Zarë'qu's intrigue was the visible turning of his mouth. "Not like you to brood, Vi," he said and he bit off another piece of the prune. "Now that I think of it I'd heard from the Elder that you've been hanging around Oruviçu recently. Don't tell me he's already rubbing off on you."

Immediately, Viorë'to scoffed like an irritated teenager. "As if..."

Zarë'qu chuckled.

"I just wanted to hear your thoughts on something," she admitted.

"Wow, you came all the way down here just to talk to little old me? I'm flattered."

Viorë'to smirked. "Don't let it get to your head. I'm just on my way back to my post after reporting to the Elder about something else. That Katruskik Alliance crossed into Lenora recently." She looked away contemplatively, and her hands rose to her hips. "Their methods are shady."

"But that's not what you want to pick my brain about, I'm guessing." Zarë'qu extended his half-eaten prune to the sun, so that the fruit and star made a complete shape. "So I wonder...maybe what you really wanna talk to me about has something to do with the boy Çaru'qu calls to?"

Viorë'to turned on him, stunned. "How did you —?!"

Zarë'qu laughed openly. "Come on, you don't think I'm always just here, do you? I'm part of the Order, just like you. The Elder requires me to make my rounds across the Empire as well. Plus, I figured that you'd be a little put off by it."

Viorë'to pouted, but she didn't respond.

"I saw him, you know. That boy. Not long ago...and not far from here, actually. It was quite uncanny." Zarë'qu looked into the valleys that rolled out beneath them. "While images of Zion can only be found on old temple walls these days, there's no mistaking that that kid looks just like him. Keeps eclectic company just as well: Avats…and humans. But that makes sense. He lives in a Liberation Front after all."

Viorë'to bristled and turned aside.

Zarë'qu noticed.

"Zarë'qu…" Viorë'to loosened just a bit, but her voice was tense. "You don't think it's true, do you? That Çaru'qu would actually call to the descendant of…of a *human.*" Her voice thickened as she uttered the word, as if it turned her stomach. "And not just any human."

"Hm." Zarë'qu didn't really consider her concerns. Or, perhaps it was better to say that he simply wasn't troubled by them. "But he's also a descendant of an Avat. And not just any Avat. I gotta say" — crossing his arms, he ambled along the edge of the cliff behind her — "I was pretty excited to see him passing through my region, of all places. I even got to see my nephew with him. Of course, the guy was out cold." Zarë'qu shook his head and raised his shoulders. "But after what they pulled off in the mines, who can blame him?"

Viorë'to bit her tongue.

"You might've heard this from Oruviçu already," Zarë'qu started, turning his head to her, for the tension that surrounded her was as thick as the aether, "but if this really is the solution that Çaru'qu has called for, then we have no right to complain. After all, the alternative…" His eyes inched across the surrounding landscape, with its sprawling fields, jagged peaks, and speckles of human civilization. "Well, no matter what side you're on, it's not a pleasant option."

Viorë'to considered that. At length, she spoke up. "'In the face of what may come…biases will be of no use to us'."

Zarë'qu bobbed his head, considering that. "Sounds like something Oruviçu would say."

"Because he did say it." Viorë'to's mask covered her scowl. "Even if he has no right to. That hypocrite…"

"Well…like him or not," Zarë'qu shrugged, "Commander Oruviçu has always been one to put duty before his own feelings. Makes sense, then, that the Elder would appoint him as our leader."

Zarë'qu watched her for a moment. "So? What're you gonna

do?"

Viorë'to considered his question, or at least the options that her mind immediately provided her with. She opened her mouth to confess to one of them but, deciding against it, she pressed her lips together.

"Aw, c'mon, Viorë'to! I'd think that the answer would be obvious, given that Çaru'qu himself has finally started callin' the shots this time around. That's history in the making all on its own. But it also means that we're running out of time. Fortunately, Çaru'qu's decisions haven't failed us yet — not Avats, or humans."

Viorë'to didn't answer, but Zarë'qu could tell that his words were getting through to her.

He concluded with one final thought. "So, if you wanna pick my brain on it, I say we go along with Çaru'qu's choice. And seeing as we're members of the Order of Zion, our allegiance becomes that much more clear."

Viorë'to glanced at him, then away. Looking out over the sea put the fading sunlight in her line of vision.

"Yeah," she said at last and the pinkish skyline dipped into darkness. "That's true."

Zarë'qu cocked his head. "Right? After all…" He smiled mysteriously. "Even if his blood is tainted by that of Axelius Arkania…it's our job to protect and support Zion's descendants."

Viorë'to couldn't even begin to form a counterargument. "Yeah," she said again. "You're right."

She said nothing else to him. Rather she stepped forward, as if she meant to step entirely off of the cliff that she and Zarë'qu now stood on.

Then, with a brief flash of light and a short gust of wind, she disappeared, as if to join with the fading sunlight and merge with the stars.[tv]

PAST GRUDGES
CODE: NEWCHOSEN

TALES OF ARKANIA
new episodes every 3rd Saturday

NEW THRILLS. NEW TALES.

Brand-new bonus content for *The Avat Prince* every third Saturday!

Featuring an international cast of voice talent, including award-winning VA Josh Portillo!

About the Author(ess)

Myranda V. Peterson

A young artist who wears many hats, Myranda Victoria Peterson is an author, illustrator, animator and voice director with a contagious passion for storytelling. She first started off writing plays, which her parents and friends helped her perform when she was a little girl. A self-taught artist, her creative work is heavily inspired by anime and Japanese pop culture. She creates original, high-fantasy content that aims to inspire the youth of today with themes of generosity, courage, friendship and hope.

Myranda is the founder and CEO of the independent imprint and joint animation studio House MVP and lives in Boston, where many famous, classic authors have gone before her. She hopes that one day, her name will join them!